6 Chelsea Walk

This series is a unique collaboration between three award-winning authors, Adèle Geras, Linda Newbery and Ann Turnbull, all writing about one very special house and the extraordinary girls and women who have lived there throughout history.

This collection first published in the USA in 2019 by Usborne Publishing Ltd.,
Usborne House, 83-85 Saffron Hill, London EC1N 8RT, England. www.usborne.com

Copyright © Ann Turnbull, 2007
Copyright © Adèle Geras, 2004

The rights of Ann Turnbull and Adèle Geras to be identified as the authors of these works has
been asserted by them in accordance with the Copyright, Designs and Patents Act, 1988.

Cover and inside illustrations by Tiziana Longo © Usborne Publishing, 2018.

The name Usborne and the devices ♛ 🎈 are Trade Marks of Usborne Publishing Ltd.

This is a work of fiction. The characters, incidents, and dialogues are products of the author's
imagination and are not to be construed as real. Any resemblance to actual events or persons,
living or dead, is entirely coincidental.

A CIP catalogue record for this book is available from the British Library.

JFMAMJJAS ND/19 05702/1 ISBN: 9780794548322 ALB: 9781601304841

Printed in China.

6 Chelsea Walk

1764

Girls
with a
Voice

ANN TURNBULL

USBORNE

For Roberta

Contents

6 CHELSEA WALK, 1764

Basement

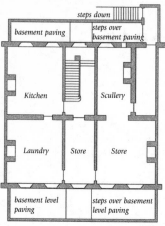

steps down

basement paving

steps over basement paving

Kitchen

Scullery

Laundry

Store

Store

basement level paving

steps over basement level paving

First-floor

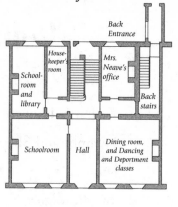

Back Entrance

House-keeper's room

Mrs. Neave's office

School-room and library

Back stairs

Schoolroom

Hall

Dining room, and Dancing and Deportment classes

Second-floor

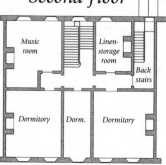

Music room

Linen-storage room

Back stairs

Dormitory

Dorm.

Dormitory

Third-floor

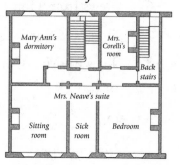

Mary Ann's dormitory

Mrs. Corelli's room

Back stairs

Mrs. Neave's suite

Sitting room

Sick room

Bedroom

Roof space

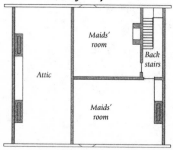

Maids' room

Back stairs

Attic

Maids' room

CHAPTER ONE

A New School

Mary Ann had read Mrs. Neave's advertisement so many times, and with such happy anticipation, that she knew it by heart:

MRS. NEAVE'S BOARDING SCHOOL
FOR YOUNG LADIES

A genteel riverside establishment in the village of
Chelsea, having the advantage of clean air and

proximity to the countryside, and yet within four miles of the City. Parents may be assured that every care is taken of our pupils, and attention paid to their manners and behavior at all times. Young ladies are taught: English, French, Arithmetic, Geography, Needlework, Comportment and Dancing; with the opportunity to take lessons in Singing and Harpsichord at a small extra cost. 21 guineas a year.

Singing and harpsichord lessons! Mary Ann could imagine nothing she would like more. And that small extra cost would easily be borne by her father, who spared no expense if it would further his children's advancement in the world. Her mother had visited Mrs. Neave's establishment and pronounced it suitable, and today, April 30 1764, Mary Ann was to leave home.

She looked out of the window and glimpsed, between rooftops and chimneys, the Thames, busy with small boats. Soon she would be there, on the river, on her way to Chelsea. Now that the moment had come she felt a rush of affection for her home, for her family and servants, the old dog Bullet with his unsteady waddle and adoring eyes, the familiar streets of the City.

Her elder sister Harriet tapped at the door and came in.

"I see you are dressed and ready." She joined Mary Ann at the window. "Are you nervous?"

"Yes." It would be strange to be away from home, sharing every moment with other girls. And what would those girls be like? Most of them would be older than her: "refined, elegant young ladies," Mrs. Neave had told her mother. "Will they all be very grand, do you think?"

"Of course not! They'll be girls like you. You'll soon make friends."

Harriet smiled. She smiled often these days. Her own schooldays were behind her and she had recently become engaged to be married. Mary Ann thought her fiancé, Mr. Philip Browne, rather old and dull, but she supposed Harriet must like him; certainly Harriet liked the prospect of having a home and servants of her own.

"We'll write to each other," said Harriet.

"Yes! And I'll write to George."

Her brother was at a boarding school in Hertfordshire. They were close in age and she missed him.

"Mary Ann!"

Her mother's voice sounded from the floor below; and Amy, their lady's maid, came back into the room to check Mary Ann's dress and hair before allowing her downstairs to be inspected.

The sisters went down together to the drawing room, where their mother was waiting.

"Oh!" she exclaimed. "How grownup you look, Mary Ann!"

Mary Ann's fair hair was drawn back from her face and arranged in neat curls. Her blue cotton gown (expensive but not showy, as befitted a merchant's schoolgirl daughter) was worn over a hooped frame, and this, together with stays boned at front and back, forced her to stand up straight under her mother's scrutiny.

Her mother turned her around and nodded approval. "Yes. You'll do well. And now we must go. Tom is waiting downstairs with your trunk."

They all went out into the courtyard. The servants – Sarah and Betty – came out to wish Mary Ann well, and Harriet kissed her goodbye. Bullet wagged his tail and pushed a damp nose against her hand. Her father, who went early to the coffee house to do business, had already said his farewell. Now their serving man Tom lifted the trunk and the three of them set off on the short walk to the pier at Old Swan Stairs.

Tom soon found them a boatman, and helped both mother and daughter aboard. The boat rocked alarmingly as Mary Ann stepped in, and it was no easy task to arrange her hooped skirts around herself as she sat down. She knew that getting in and out of boats and carriages gracefully was one of the many skills she would be expected to learn at Mrs. Neave's school.

She pulled her wrap around her shoulders as the boat moved out into the center of the river. They left the City and traveled west, passing Whitehall, Westminster and the Houses of Parliament. Then came a great bend in the river, the buildings on the shore were less densely packed and she began to see fields beyond them. Mary Ann thought they must be nearly there, but it still seemed an age before the boatman pulled in at a small dock on a tree-lined bank, and she saw beyond it a road with a row of tall terraced houses facing the river.

"There is Chelsea Walk," said her mother.

They disembarked and climbed the shallow steps to the road, Tom following with the trunk.

Mrs. Neave's establishment was at Number Six: a large five-story house of red brick with tall wrought-iron gates.

Mary Ann looked up. She had an impression of many rows of windows, all watching her as she shook down the crumpled layers of her skirts and began to pick her way across the muddy road. Beyond the gates was a short garden and a flight of steps leading to the front door.

Her mother took her hand and squeezed it. She led Mary Ann in through the gateway and up the steps, and knocked at the door. A maid – a dark-eyed, handsome girl – let them into the hall and then went to fetch her mistress.

Mary Ann stood on the black and white tiled floor and looked around at the lofty space. The hall was paneled in wood, and there were several closed doors – one with a murmur of voices behind it – and an archway leading to the back where a great staircase with polished wooden boards led up to a tall window on the half landing, then turned and carried on upwards. She felt very small.

"Mrs. Giffard!"

"Mrs. Neave."

A woman of about her mother's age had appeared. She was dressed in dark blue silk and looked, Mary Ann thought, rather severe compared to Mama in her striped yellow gown and little tilted straw hat. The two women nodded politely to each other.

"And Mary Ann," said Mrs. Neave, turning to her. "Welcome to our school."

Mary Ann made a small, nervous curtsy.

"You will take tea, Mrs. Giffard, before you return to the City?"

Her mother accepted, and Mrs. Neave called to the maid. "Tea, Jenny, in my office. And tell Mrs. Giffard's man to take the young lady's trunk to the rear entrance."

Jenny disappeared into the back area of the building.

Nearby, in the hall, a door opened and several girls of about Mary Ann's own age came out, carrying books. Mrs. Neave stopped one of them – a friendly-looking girl with auburn curls.

"Sophia, this is Mary Ann Giffard. Mary Ann, Sophia Hammond."

The girls nodded to each other, and Mary Ann felt Sophia's eyes taking in every detail of her appearance.

"Sophia will take you around the school and show you where you are to sleep. But first: say goodbye to your mother."

Mary Ann turned to her mother. She wished they did not have to say goodbye so publicly. Her mother's eyes were pink, as if she was holding back tears, and Mary Ann felt her own eyes pricking. She submitted to a brief kiss, then stepped brusquely away.

"You'll be home for Whitsun," her mother said, as if to reassure herself. "Now, be sure I hear well of you. And write to us…"

"I will," said Mary Ann, retreating, aware that Sophia was observing the exchange with interest.

When the other girl moved away Mary Ann was glad to follow her and leave the two women to discuss finance over their tea.

Sophia waved a hand at the room she had just left, and from which people were still coming out.

"The downstairs rooms are the main classrooms, and the dining room is here too." She briefly opened a door across the hall, and Mary Ann saw two long tables. "That room at the back is the office, where your mother is taking tea. Let's go upstairs. I'll show you the music room."

"Oh!" exclaimed Mary Ann. "A music room!"

"Do you like music?"

"I do. It's quite my favorite occupation. I'm to have harpsichord and singing lessons."

Sophia looked pleased. "I have music lessons too. Mrs. Corelli is our singing teacher and Mr. Ashton teaches harpsichord."

She walked ahead of Mary Ann around the turn of the grand staircase, and Mary Ann thought what a big house this was, though rather dark and old-fashioned with its unpainted wood paneling.

"Most of the rooms on this floor are dormitories

for the older girls," said Sophia. "But over here is the music room."

No one was in the room, so they were able to look around. There were shelves of books, music stands, flutes and other wind instruments, and a harpsichord.

"Do you have an instrument at home?" asked Sophia.

"A virginal. There is no space for anything bigger. But my sister and I both play."

"Sometimes Mr. Ashton plays for us," said Sophia. "He is a wonderful musician – and quite *divinely* handsome. Half the older girls are in love with him." She sighed theatrically. "But he's married, and quite old: twenty-eight at least."

"My sister's fiancé is twenty-eight," said Mary Ann.

"Oh! Your sister is getting married! When?"

"Next year, or the one after."

"And is she greatly in love?"

Mary Ann frowned. "I don't think so. But Mother says love is not to be recommended and that girls may do better without it."

"I shall insist on being in love when *I* marry," said Sophia.

"I don't think I want to marry at all," said Mary Ann.

Sophia's eyes opened wide. "But you would not wish to be a spinster?"

"I want to be a singer – at the opera." Mary Ann did not often tell anyone this, for it was difficult to convey how strongly she wished it, but Sophia seemed to invite confidences. She added, "Of course my parents say it is not a respectable profession."

"But you might catch the attention of a lord – and marry him! Several famous singers have. Think of that!"

She went on to ask Mary Ann about her family, and to talk about her own: her two younger brothers and baby sister; their house in Holborn; their spaniel.

"Come upstairs," she said. "I'll show you our room. Your trunk should be there by now."

They went up yet another flight to another paneled hall full of closed doors.

"Those rooms at the front are Mrs. Neave's own apartment," said Sophia, "and Mrs. Corelli has this room by the stairs. Our dormitory is here. It's above the music room."

She opened the door into a plain room with four beds, neatly made, a few chairs, and a washstand with jug, bowl and mirror. Mary Ann's trunk was standing in front of the fireplace.

"Your clothes go in that cupboard by the door," said Sophia. She eyed the trunk, and Mary Ann knew she wanted to be there when it was opened.

She saw that the bed in the far corner seemed to be hers; the others had chairs or shelves with small things – a prayer book, a handkerchief, a locket – on them.

"Who else sleeps here?" she asked.

"Lucy Stanley, over there." Sophia indicated a bed set a little separate from the others, in the space behind the door. "And Phoebe Merrill, here, next to me. You may have the corner bed. We are the youngest girls in the school. Lucy and I are thirteen; we have been here since January. And Phoebe is twelve. She came a few weeks ago. How old are you?"

"Twelve," said Mary Ann. "Thirteen in September."

Sophia smiled. "We shall all be great friends, I'm sure. Phoebe – well, everyone likes Phoebe. And Lucy is our smart one; we are quite in awe of her." She glanced again at Mary Ann's trunk. "You should unpack soon or your clothes will be creased. I'll show you where they go."

She opened a cabinet beside the door, revealing shelves and a few hooks for hanging clothes. Most of the space was taken up by full-skirted gowns and petticoats.

"There are two hooks here," said Sophia, "and these lower shelves. Cloaks and hats go in the other cabinet. Have you brought much?"

"No."

Mary Ann lifted the lid of the trunk. Her nightgown lay on top and she removed it and laid it on her bed.

Sophia watched as she took out two cotton gowns, several shifts, stays, and a gown of pale green silk with a yellow petticoat – "for special occasions," she explained, wondering if there would be any.

Sophia stroked the silk admiringly and found a place for it in the cabinet. "You might wear that if we go to Ranelagh Gardens," she said.

"Ranelagh? To the Pleasure Gardens?" Mary Ann could scarcely believe she might go *there*. She had heard all about Chelsea's famous Ranelagh Gardens, where concerts were held on summer evenings in the Rotunda – "with a roof, so that it may be used even in bad weather," her sister had said – and where the gentry came to mingle and be seen.

"Mrs. Neave likes to take some of her girls to a concert there each summer," said Sophia.

"Oh! I should *so* love to go! Have you ever been there?"

"No. But the older girls tell me it is not to be missed."

From far below came the sound of someone ringing a bell.

"Dinner!" said Sophia. "Also not to be missed. Come and meet the others."

CHAPTER TWO

Nymphs and Shepherds

The dining room was full of voices, movement, rustling skirts. Mary Ann felt eyes on her: the eyes of the teachers who had taken their places at the ends of each table, and those of passing girls. She felt nervous, and was glad of Sophia's presence.

"Stand here," said Sophia, "next to me."

They were at the lower table, nearest the door and the kitchen entrance. A teacher stood at the end, and opposite Mary Ann and Sophia were two girls who Sophia introduced in a whisper: "Lucy and Phoebe."

Both girls smiled. Phoebe was pretty, fair and small. Lucy, a taller, quiet-looking girl, had a shy manner.

A hush fell on the room, and Mrs. Neave, at the far end, said grace. Mary Ann joined in the murmured "Amen," and there was a scraping of chairs as they all sat down and the servants moved into the room carrying dishes.

Mary Ann scarcely noticed the food, except to watch that she did not eat too fast for good manners; or too slowly; or reach for things across the table. Several dishes passed by her because she was too shy to ask for them. The teacher at the end called back a dish of carp and told Mary Ann, "Try this. It's good."

Sophia turned to the teacher: "Mrs. Corelli, Mary Ann is to have singing lessons with you. She is quite in *love* with music and wishes to become an opera singer."

Mary Ann blushed and looked at her plate. She

hadn't expected her confidence to Sophia to be passed on so publicly. And whatever would Mrs. Corelli think? Would she be dismissive, like Mary Ann's parents?

But Mrs. Corelli did not look surprised or disapproving. "I know Mary Ann is to have lessons," she said, "and I shall hear her sing this afternoon, after our comportment lesson."

But before Comportment came half an hour of French Conversation with Mrs. Neave.

"*Je ne comprends pas*," whispered Sophia as they followed a group of older girls into the front classroom. "Our most useful phrase."

"Here's another," said Lucy, pretending boredom: "*Le Français m'ennuie à mourir*."

They laughed. But Lucy, it turned out, was excellent at French: Mrs. Neave's best pupil. She could both speak and write the language well. Mary Ann's French was limited to what she had learned at her day school, and she struggled to keep up. She was relieved that Phoebe also seemed to be having trouble.

Phoebe preferred their next lesson. The anxiety left her face as they returned to the dining room, where the center had been cleared of furniture to make room for Comportment and Dancing with Mrs. Corelli.

Mrs. Corelli was a large woman who moved with surprising lightness and grace. She was dressed dramatically in an emerald green gown that Mary Ann much admired.

Mary Ann had thought learning how to stand up and sit down in a hooped skirt, how to curtsy, how to walk, would be boring, but Mrs. Corelli made it fun.

"Imagine, girls," she said, "that you are out walking in the street, wearing a hooped skirt. If you bounce along, like this" – she began walking in a jaunty way, and they giggled – "your skirt will set up a rhythm of its own and you will not be able to control it, especially in a strong wind. And what if you sit down?"

She bounced down onto a chair so that her skirt stuck up at the front, revealing striped stockings which

Mary Ann suspected she had worn especially to make them laugh.

They promenaded around the room, careful to hold themselves erect, then practiced sitting down and standing up, and taking a man's arm – Mrs. Corelli acting the part of the man.

"Lightly, child!" she exclaimed, when it was Mary Ann's turn. "Do not *clutch*."

Mary Ann was embarrassed. It did not seem to her at all a comfortable way to walk, and she hoped no man would ever offer her his arm. She was relieved when they finished the lesson with a dance: a minuet. There was a harpsichord in the corner of the room, and Mrs. Corelli played, glancing up to watch them. The older girls took the man's part, and Mary Ann found herself dancing with a tall girl named Emma whose limp hold made her own steps uncertain. She watched Phoebe, who looked as if she was born to dance.

"Oh, I love the minuet!" Phoebe exclaimed afterward. "I can't wait to be old enough to go to balls!"

There was now a break from lessons, and the girls, who all looked pink and hot, fanned themselves as they lined up for lemonade. Mrs. Corelli took two glasses and summoned Mary Ann.

"We shall take these up to the music room and I'll hear you sing."

"Oh! Now?"

Mary Ann was alarmed. What would Mrs. Corelli think of her singing? And *what* would she ask her to sing? Perhaps something difficult.

But when they reached the music room Mrs. Corelli looked through a collection of songs and asked, "Now, what do you know? 'Nymphs and Shepherds'? 'On Greenland's Coast'?"

"Oh, yes! Both. I mean – yes, I like 'Nymphs and Shepherds.'"

"Good."

She put the music on the stand and sat down at the harpsichord and began to play. Mary Ann came in on time, but tentatively. It was a while before she gained confidence and sang louder.

"*In this grove,*

In this grove let's sport and play,

Let's sport and play…"

She was enjoying herself now, and as she continued she almost forgot she was being tested.

"*Sacred to ease and happy love,*

To music, to dancing and to poetry…"

When she reached the end she saw that Mrs. Corelli was pleased.

"You have a lovely natural voice," she said. "Soprano. I'm glad you going to take lessons. You will learn to control your breathing and to sing from *here* –" She put a hand on her midriff. "You will have lessons with me once a week and you will also join the choir. And I'm sure Mrs. Neave will want you to take part in our concert in September."

"A concert!"

"Every September we invite parents and visitors to the school. There is a display of work – needlework, drawing and such – and a concert with recitation, singing and playing."

"I would love to be in the concert," said Mary Ann. And she thought: perhaps, if I sing well, Mama will believe that I could become an opera singer.

She knew her father was less antagonistic to this idea than Mama. He was a bit of a singer himself, and it was his mother – her Grandmama Giffard – from whom Mary Ann had inherited her voice, and who had taken her to the opera for the first time and inspired in her the ambition to perform. She remembered how they had sat high up in the gallery and seen the singers far below on the candlelit stage – a jeweled tableau in a circle of light – and heard their voices soaring. Grandmama Giffard had died last year, but Mary Ann remembered her with love and gratitude.

"We will try 'Nymphs and Shepherds' again," said Mrs. Corelli. "But first, let us talk about breathing…"

Mary Ann left after half an hour and joined the others, who were reading around the group: a self-improvement text on the subject of modesty.

Later, after supper, lagging a little behind the other three on their way to the dormitory, she had reached the first floor when she heard singing. Someone was singing 'Nymphs and Shepherds' in an easy, absent-minded way, humming over forgotten words – and she had the feeling that whoever it was had heard her practicing with Mrs. Corelli and picked up the song by ear. The voice was a woman's, untrained, clear and pleasant, like those of some of the ballad singers Mary Ann loved to hear in the streets near her home.

Who could it be? The sound did not come from the music room but from a room next to the back stairs – a room Sophia hadn't bothered to mention.

She did not dare open the door; and when she hurried to join the other three on the third floor she was caught up in a flurry of gossip and giggles and forgot to ask them about it.

CHAPTER THREE

Jenny

Monday, 28th May, 1764

Dear Harriet,

I can scarcely believe it is already a month since I came here to Chelsea. I told you in my last letter how very much I liked the school and I am still of the same mind. Mrs. Corelli is so kind as to say that she thinks well of my singing and that I am developing a stronger voice already. Mr. Ashton, who teaches the harpsichord, is also pleased with my efforts. He takes us for Music and also Mathematics.

I am the best of friends with the three girls I share a room with. All four of us take harpsichord lessons, and Sophia and I are both in the choir. Sophia is full of gossip and plans: she is our leader. Phoebe is amiable and follows Sophia's view in everything. As for Lucy, Sophia teases her that she is so brilliant she will not get a husband. Lucy has a collection of shells and minerals which she keeps in a case under her bed (to the annoyance of the maids who try to sweep there). Although she is shy, she is witty and often makes us laugh.

I have written to Mama and expect she has told you that we read together in class every day, and write essays, and Mrs. Neave also teaches us Geography. There is a splendid globe, like the one Papa bought for George, but larger. We do needlework, which I like less, but Phoebe produces exquisite work; her stitches are so fine they can scarcely be seen.

We also go out to get fresh air, and on these occasions we are expected to behave in a ladylike manner; only sometimes we are so excited that it is difficult not to exclaim or dart about. Last Saturday, on our half-day of school, a group of us went to the Chelsea Bun House, which sells the most delicious sugared buns and cakes — you would love it, Harriet — but Lucy was even more delighted over the collection of curios and antiques which forms a small museum within the shop. We saw some extraordinary objects there, among them preserved squid, and fossils, and a stuffed lizard.

On Sundays we walk to church in a line. The church is nearby, in Chelsea Walk, and is ancient; it has been here since Chelsea's beginnings. Inside, we listen to very long sermons. They are exceedingly dull. But we behave ourselves well and make a good impression on our neighbors, and that pleases Mrs. Neave. Of course we also sing hymns, which I enjoy.

There is another person here who likes to sing: one of the maids. Her name is Jenny. I heard her singing "Nymphs and Shepherds."

Mary Ann paused, and put down her pen. Perhaps it would be best not to write too much about Jenny. Harriet would undoubtedly share the letter with Mama, and their mother might not like the idea of Mary Ann making a particular friend of one of the maids.

She remembered her first evening, when she had heard the singing, and how she had seen Jenny the next morning, coming out of the room on the second floor, her arms full of clean, folded bed linen. The open doorway behind her had revealed a storage room containing shelves and baskets and a linen press. Jenny was humming to herself, and Mary Ann had known at once that here was her singer from the night before.

Without thinking, she exclaimed, "Oh! It was you!" The maid looked startled, and Mary Ann explained,

"I heard you singing yesterday: 'Nymphs and Shepherds.' I'd been practicing it with Mrs. Corelli."

Jenny smiled. "I like to learn the young ladies' songs. They're different from the ballads I hear in the streets."

"Do you come from Chelsea?"

"Yes. My mother has a room on the waterfront, by the ferry. There's a tavern near our house, the Half Moon: I sing there some nights. And at the Duke of York."

Mary Ann was impressed. Jenny was a performer! She much admired the girl's looks: her dark eyes and tall, slender figure. She thought Jenny a better-looking girl than any of the young ladies at the school. She said shyly, "I should like to hear you."

Jenny laughed. "Oh, I don't think so, Miss – not in a tavern." She shifted her bundle of linen and said, "I must see to my work, or Mrs. Price will be after me."

"The housekeeper?"

"Yes."

She knocked at one of the dormitory doors opposite and, receiving no answer, went in.

It was a while before they spoke to one another again, but Jenny always acknowledged the younger girl with a smile, and Mary Ann felt that they had become friends. A week or two later, when the choir had been talking about Ranelagh Gardens, Mary Ann asked Jenny if she had ever been there.

"Oh, yes, Miss! Not as a visitor. That costs two and sixpence; even more on firework nights. But my cousin Nick plays the fiddle, and sometimes he'll go in and play for the crowds in the gardens. Last time he took me with him and I sang. We made a hatful of money before the officials moved us on. You'd love the Gardens, Miss; all the great folk go there. And the lights! It's like Paradise…"

Mary Ann brought her attention back to her letter.

I'll be home in less than two weeks, for Whitsun, she wrote. *And George too. We shall all have so much to tell each other. I am glad to hear your news from home, and*

especially that Papa expects success from his new venture.
If he is in good spirits when I come home, do you think he'll
take us to the Tower to see the animals? I do so love to go.

Till then, dear Harriet, I remain,

Your devoted sister,

Mary Ann Giffard

CHAPTER FOUR

Two Prodigies

The girls all went home for a week's vacation at Whitsun. Sophia, tossing dresses and stockings into her bag, made a great show of despair at the prospect of being parted from her friends.

"I don't know how I shall *endure* vacation without you all! My brothers are *odious* and delight in provoking me. The week will seem far too long."

Mary Ann knew Sophia well enough by now not to

take all this too seriously. And Lucy said, "Well, I shall be glad to go home and see my cats and not have to think about school for a week."

"Oh, Lucy! You are heartless!" protested Sophia. "Mary Ann, will *your* brother be home? Is he as maddening as my two?"

Mary Ann said yes, he was, because that seemed to be the thing to say. In fact, she rather enjoyed George's company and had always been closer to him than to Harriet, who was seven years older than her.

"Lucy is lucky to be an only child." Phoebe, who also suffered from brothers, was rolling stockings into pairs.

A bell rang far below, signaling breakfast, and all four of them shrieked in alarm and flung a few more items into their bags before hurrying downstairs.

A buzz of chatter enlivened the group as they filed into the dining room.

"Did you hear about those extraordinary children from – where was it? – somewhere in Austria?"

"Salzburg," said an older girl near Mary Ann. "The Mozarts."

"Such amazing musicians!"

Mary Ann listened eagerly to the gossip. She heard that there were two Mozart children, a boy of eight and a girl of twelve, and both were such gifted musicians that they had taken London by storm. They had arrived in the city with their parents only five weeks ago and had already been invited twice to the palace to play for the King and Queen.

"Of course the King loves music, and the Queen sings…"

"The King was enchanted with them, especially the little boy –"

"They say the boy composes and plays his own works. At such a young age! It is amazing."

"And the girl plays the harpsichord with brilliance…"

It seemed that there had been a concert at Spring Garden on Tuesday at which these "prodigies," as their father described them, had performed.

"Oh! I wish we could have gone!" exclaimed Mary Ann.

Lucy widened her eyes. "At half a guinea a ticket? I think not."

But after breakfast Mrs. Neave asked all the music students to stay behind. She told them about another concert – one they might be able to afford.

"I am arranging our annual visit to Ranelagh," she said. "There is to be a charity concert there in aid of a new hospital on Friday the 29th of June. The music is sure to be popular pieces that you will know, and this will be an opportunity – the first for some of you – to see Ranelagh Gardens. I shall inquire about tickets after next week's vacation, when I know how many of you are coming. If you wish to be included in our party, please ask your parents for five shillings, and bring the money with you when you return to school. Don't forget."

As if we would, thought Mary Ann. And Sophia said, "Let's all go! It'll be such fun!"

"Don't let Mrs. Neave hear you say 'fun,'" said Lucy, and Sophia put a hand over her mouth and made a face. "Fun" was a word used by young men about town, not by young ladies.

"What fun!" exclaimed George, when Mary Ann met him at home later that day and told him about the concert. "Ranelagh is all the rage, I hear."

"*Everyone* will be there," Mary Ann agreed, and sighed theatrically, Sophia-style. She meant everyone of consequence: the gentry, perhaps even royalty. "It will be quite divine!"

"Oh! *Quite* divine!" George, grinning, hopped out of reach as she went to hit him. They had all been teasing her, ever since she got home, about her new way of talking. She'd picked it up from Sophia without noticing, and now it had become second nature.

Her mother did not object.

"I'd rather Mary Ann spoke in that way than copied some of the girls at her old day school," she told a smirking George and Harriet. "And see how well she looks, and how she carries herself! I'm pleased with the change in her."

They were all impressed with the improvement in Mary Ann's harpsichord playing, and with Mrs. Corelli's comments on her singing. Mary Ann had chattered all the way home about the school, the teachers, her friends, and her music lessons.

"I do so love being there," she said. "And Mama, I need five shillings for the concert at Ranelagh! And my shoes are shabby – the ones I wore last summer…"

"George needs books and new clothes too," said her mother, "and Harriet must have a whole new wardrobe now she is engaged to Mr. Browne."

But none of this was a problem. When her father came home, Mary Ann dropped him a perfect curtsy, and he laughed with pleasure and took her hand and then scooped her into a hug. "My little girl! You are quite a lady already!"

He approved a visit to Cheapside for "shopping," as the ladies liked to call it.

"When the *Calliope* comes in – any day now – we'll be rich," he said. "You'll be in fine feather then, Harriet; more than a match for any son of Walter Browne." He winked above Mary Ann's head at her mother. "This'll show the old lady."

His wife gave a little shake of her head to silence him. But Mary Ann knew what he meant. "The old lady" was her other grandmother, her mother's mother, Mrs. Eleanor Causey, who was now a widow and lived in Kensington. Grandfather Causey had been a lawyer, and he and his wife had always disapproved of John Giffard because he gambled and took financial risks. They believed he could not give their daughter the security and respectability she deserved. Susan Causey had married him against their wishes, and had never been forgiven. So the Giffard children rarely saw their grandmother and Mrs. Causey was almost a stranger to them.

Their mother and Harriet began talking about silks and muslins, and which colors might suit Harriet's complexion. Mary Ann and George went down to the kitchen, chatted with the servants, wheedled some treats from Cook, and fussed over old Bullet. They ended up in the small garden, where George climbed the apple tree and Mary Ann, despite her stiff skirts, followed him. They sat companionably, eating their pastries.

"Papa's in high spirits," said George. "Better make the most of it."

"What's this ship?"

Mary Ann did not really understand what her father did for a living. There was nothing to see, no merchandise to handle. His dealings involved investments and returns, and sometimes losses, and his mood would go up or down in tune with them.

"The *Calliope*?" said George. "She went out to West Africa last year. I don't know what the cargo was, but he was persuaded it was a good investment.

She's on her way back from the Caribbean now."

"From the *Caribbean*?" Mary Ann had been making good use of the globe in her Geography lessons at school. "But you said the ship went to Africa."

"They buy slaves in Africa," George explained, "and sell them in the Caribbean. They're needed to work on the sugar plantations."

"How cruel – to seize people."

"They are not seized; not by Englishmen. Other Africans sell them to the traders. Papa told me."

Mary Ann thought of Lady Fanshawe, who lived at Number Five, Chelsea Walk. She had a black servant, a boy of about George's age. But that boy was not a slave, was he? He could not be, surely, not in England.

For a while she remained troubled about the *Calliope*, but before long it went out of her mind as she was caught up in a round of social events. They took tea with the Brownes. They went to the Tower of London's menagerie and saw lions, elephants, camels and a zebra. They went to Cheapside and chose materials to be made up into clothes for Harriet and George and they ordered new summer shoes (pale soft leather with gilt buckles) for Mary Ann. One fine sunny day they made up a party with Mr. Browne and his sisters and walked in Kensington Gardens; and Mary Ann thought of her grandmother, who lived alone nearby, and wondered if she regretted the rift with her family.

The warm weather continued after Mary Ann returned to school. She became aware, almost for the first time, of the garden at the rear of the house. It was larger than the one at home, and laid out with paths and shrubs and sweet-smelling herbs that released their scent when her skirts brushed against them. Some steps there led down to the basement where the kitchen servants worked.

Her friend Jenny always entered the house that way, along with the other servants. But Jenny spent much of her time in the main part of the house, cleaning the rooms, bed-making, folding and sorting laundry.

One hot afternoon, a day or two after their return, when the girls were sketching in the garden, Mary Ann was sent indoors to fetch her straw hat. She ran upstairs. The second floor landing was deserted, but the door to the linen-storage room was ajar, and she saw a flicker of movement inside. That must be Jenny! She knocked, and pushed the door open at the same time.

"Oh!"

Jenny was behind the door, and both girls jumped, startled. But Jenny flushed scarlet – as if caught in a guilty act.

Mary Ann took in the scene. There was a basket on the floor – evidently Jenny's own basket, for her gloves and shawl were inside it. Jenny had been crouching, about to push something – a bundle of linen – under the shawl. She stood trapped, holding the linen. It was obvious that she'd intended to steal it.

Mary Ann, shocked and disillusioned, stared and felt herself going red in her turn.

Jenny unrolled the bundle, revealing it to be two pillowcases.

"Please, don't tell Mrs. Neave!" she begged.

CHAPTER FIVE

Maria Anna

"But – why?"

Mary Ann's disappointment in Jenny felt like a blow. She'd thought so highly of her. She did not want to believe her friend was a thief.

"It's my sister." Jenny folded the pillowcases and replaced them on a shelf. "She's ill – wasting away – spends most of her time in bed. And our bed linen at home is coarse stuff…"

At once Mary Ann felt both sorry and relieved. Jenny only wanted some comfort for her sister. She was not really a thief – or not such a bad one.

"You won't tell?" Jenny asked again.

"No…no, of course not," said Mary Ann, adding awkwardly, "I hope your sister will soon be well," although she thought "wasting away" didn't sound hopeful at all.

"Bless you!" Jenny's face cleared.

Mary Ann remembered her sun hat, and turned to go upstairs. Her faith in Jenny was restored – although since Jenny's basket was so close to the shelf with the pillowcases on it, she could not help wondering if they would find their way into it again.

But that was not her concern; and she had other things to think of. At the end of the week Mrs. Neave received the tickets and program for the concert at Ranelagh Gardens. The program gave details of the music to be played.

"A favorite chorus in *Acis and Galatea*," she told the

girls, "'O the Pleasure of the Plains'…the Song and Chorus in *Alexander's Feast*…and a surprise, which I think will please you: the two children of Mr. Mozart will perform on the harpsichord and organ –"

She must have known from the intake of breath that went around that this was what interested the girls most.

She read aloud to them from the program: "The celebrated and astonishing Master Mozart will perform several fine select pieces of his own composition… which have already given the highest pleasure, delight and surprise to the greatest judges of music in England and Italy," she looked up, "…and they say that Master Mozart is the most amazing genius that has appeared in any age…"

"I cannot wait to see him!" Sophia exclaimed.

The four of them were in their dormitory, trying on their best gowns and considering whether anything new needed to be urgently requested from home.

"And *her*!" said Mary Ann. "I want to see *Miss* Mozart. They say she sings and plays the harpsichord, and she is just our age."

"I heard she is very pretty," said Phoebe. "And that Master Mozart is so small he has to sit on a cushion and even then he can scarcely reach the keys."

"How sweet!"

"And we'll hear *Acis and Galatea*," said Sophia. "I love that chorus."

She broke into song, and Mary Ann joined her:

"*O the pleasure of the plains!*

Happy nymphs and happy swains…"

Mrs. Corelli put her head around the half-open door. "You're in good voice, girls! Would you like to learn some more music from *Acis and Galatea* before we go to Ranelagh?"

"Oh, yes!" Mary Ann and Sophia agreed. And Phoebe, twirling in her sea-green gown, exclaimed, "Mrs. Corelli, we are *so* excited! Will we be able to walk in the gardens at dusk and see the lights?"

"We will," said Mrs. Corelli, "if we have good weather."

The weather was kind to them. The girls and their teachers, dressed in silk gowns and furnished with fans for the heat in the Rotunda and light shawls to protect them from the evening air, made their way two-by-two along the riverside path to the dock. There they embarked in two boats and, chattering all the way, were taken to the river entrance of Ranelagh. It was a voyage of less than a mile and took no more than ten minutes, but for Mary Ann, as they approached the famous gardens, it was one she knew she would always remember. She gazed out at the river, glinting in the sunlight and crowded with small boats. They passed the waterfront gate of the Physic Garden and the majestic steps and gates of the Royal Hospital, and in no time were in a line of boats waiting to disembark at Ranelagh.

"Oh!" exclaimed Mary Ann. "The temple!"

Inside the gardens, not far from the gates, a Grecian temple of white stone stood among trees. This was the Temple of Pan; the older girls had told them about it. Gentlemen and ladies, festive in bright summer clothes, were strolling along the paths and in and out of the temple.

It took a while for the two boatloads of girls and teachers – sixteen people in all – to come ashore. Mrs. Corelli drew the girls to the side while Mrs. Neave showed the tickets to the official at the gates; and then they were inside, walking in pairs – Mary Ann was with Lucy – along a gravel path that led first to the Temple of Pan. This proved to be less mysterious at close quarters. It contained stone seats and was clearly a meeting point, with people coming and going and greeting each other with bows and cries of delight. The path led on beneath shady trees – elms and yews – toward the formal gardens nearer the house. The Rotunda could be glimpsed through the trees, looking like some monument of Ancient Rome. They passed a lawn cut in an odd shape – "an octagon," said Lucy – and a flower garden full of lilies and roses which Mrs. Neave insisted they stop to admire, although Mary Ann longed to move on.

In front of the Rotunda was an ornamental canal with what seemed to be a Chinese pagoda on it; but as they came closer this was revealed to be an elaborate roofed bridge painted in red, blue and gold and with space for people to gather on or wander about. All the younger girls wanted to cross the bridge, but some of the older ones affected boredom and walked around the path to meet them. The bridge and all the walks were full of people, and Sophia commented continually on the fashions and hairstyles.

"I do so admire that gray hair powder," she sighed. "I long to have my hair powdered, but Mama says I must wait till I am grown up. Oh! *Mes amies, regardez* that gown!"

But Mary Ann and Lucy were caught up in amazement at the sight of the Rotunda with its great circle of windows, high up, and an arcade running all around the building.

Mrs. Neave ushered them toward one of the grand entrances. They passed between two great pillars into a central space that took Mary Ann's breath away: a huge circular room hung with chandeliers that sparkled with candlelight, and at the center a soaring column containing a fireplace – filled with flowers on this warm evening. Tilting her head back, she saw the circle of windows from the inside, high above a double ring of boxes. The orchestra, where the musicians were already warming up their instruments, was across the room. The floor was laid with matting, and this softened the sound of many footfalls as people promenaded, talking and greeting friends. There were smells of perfume, sweat, hair wax, flowers and coffee. The room was filling with more and more people, and Mary Ann felt, all around her, a gathering sense of eagerness and anticipation.

"We have two boxes on the upper tier," Mrs. Neave

said. And she shepherded her charges away from the concourse and up a staircase to a circular gallery with numbered doors.

Each box was big enough for seven girls and a teacher, with a table for their refreshments. Mary Ann was with Mrs. Corelli, who sat with three of the older girls while the younger ones squeezed past to sit in a row at the front: Sophia, Phoebe, Mary Ann and Lucy. From up here they had a view side-on to the orchestra and could see the musicians moving about, some talking, some seated and tuning their instruments. Behind the three tiers of orchestra seats the pipes of the organ rose to the ceiling. There was no sign yet of the Mozart children.

Below, the floor of the hall was full of people walking in sedate circles around the room. But now a few of them were beginning to move toward the first floor boxes, and Mary Ann saw that the musicians and choir had taken their places and the conductor had appeared. The performers were dressed in bright clothes, the men in powdered wigs and jackets trimmed with lace and braid, the ladies in low-necked silk gowns, their hair powdered in white or gray and entwined with jewels that winked as the light caught them.

As the music began, the people below paused to look up. Some clapped or cheered, and one or two called out to certain performers and received a wave in reply. The music was the promised chorus from *Acis and Galatea* by Mr. Handel. Mary Ann listened and watched, noting every detail of how the female singers moved and held themselves.

All the music that followed was of a familiar, cheerful kind, and received with frequent loud applause from the audience. A worthy-looking gentleman appeared and spoke about the benefits to be gained from the proposed maternity hospital and thanked people for their support; but the school party, eager for the Mozarts, paid little attention. Mrs. Neave looked in through the door of the box and asked what refreshments they would like for intermission, and went off to order tea, lemonade and bread and butter. The speaker retired, to applause.

Mary Ann, watching intently, was the first to see the Mozart family appear: the little boy, the girl, and a man who must be their father. She nudged Lucy and Phoebe on either side of her. "Look! They're here!"

More applause broke out as the Mozarts were introduced. Nannerl and Wolfgang, the children were called. The boy, Wolfgang, in a bright blue jacket, took his place at the organ: a tiny figure, dwarfed by the soaring pipes above him. He began to play a piece, they were told, of his own composition.

"Amazing!" murmured Mrs. Corelli, as the music filled the hall. "To compose such work at only eight years old!"

It was not until the second half of the concert that Miss Mozart performed. She moved to sit at the harpsichord: a slim, fair girl, straight-backed, wearing a green and white dress with a high neckline edged with coral-colored lace, her hair drawn up in tight curls and decorated with coral flowers. Mary Ann admired her looks, and when the girl began to play she realized why Mr. Mozart had described her as a "prodigy." She knew, from her own practice, how difficult the piece was, and yet this girl made it seem effortless.

When she finished, to a roar of applause, her brother took her place at the harpsichord and Nannerl sang. Her voice was clear, high and sweet: a good voice – but not as good as mine, Mary Ann realized with surprise and some pleasure. It was obvious that the harpsichord was Nannerl's forte. She joined her brother at the instrument and the two of them played a fast, demanding piece together, their hands crossing and uncrossing, their own and each other's, so fast they could scarcely be seen.

At the finale they stood up and bowed to the enthusiastic crowd. Even from this distance Mary Ann could see the little boy's impish face and the girl's demure smile. She looked around and saw all the boxes full of cheering people.

She turned to Mrs. Corelli, behind her. "Oh, I *wish* I could play like that! And sing in public! I'd love to be Nannerl – but what a strange name!"

"Yes." Mrs. Corelli smiled. "That's what her family calls her. I heard that her proper name is Maria Anna."

"Maria Anna?" Mary Ann looked across at the girl, and Lucy said, "That's Mary Ann! Like you!"

I *shall* be like Maria Anna, thought Mary Ann. I'll work and practice every day. And she imagined herself there, with the orchestra, the lights shining on her and applause sounding from all around.

The concert ended with "God Save the King," and everyone stood up and sang.

And then it was over. There was shuffling, coughing and scraping of chairs. A slow movement of people began toward the exits. When at last she emerged into the night air, Mary Ann saw that it was dark, and all the lamps had been lit in the gardens. The Chinese bridge was lit up, the lamps reflected on the water in disks of shifting light; and colored lanterns were hung from trees along the pathways. The girls gazed around, entranced.

"Girls! Stay together! Take care!" said Mrs. Neave.

The crowd emerging from the Rotunda divided, most people turning toward the King's private road, from where their carriages would take them home across Pimlico marshes to London. The school group joined those who were traveling by boat. This meant walking back along the treelined path that wound through the gardens, now lit all the way with lanterns. The brightness of the lamps made the darkness beyond them mysterious, as if the gardens had expanded to become a limitless domain. The Temple of Pan glowed white near the waterfront gates, and bright nymph-like figures in silken gowns could be seen moving inside.

The others chattered and giggled, but Mary Ann

was quiet, overcome by the wonder of the occasion. In her imagination she was onstage, Maria Anna and Mary Ann merged into one.

When they reached the house in Chelsea Walk and went inside, they were greeted by Mrs. Price with cups of chocolate and a warm fire in the dining room. Mary Ann sipped her chocolate, her mind still full of the sounds of singing, music and clapping, the glitter of the chandeliers and the sheen of silk. Mrs. Neave passed her a small printed card: one of the tickets for the concert. Each of the girls had one.

"A souvenir," said Mrs. Neave.

The ticket was illustrated with an engraving. It showed a woman – a goddess, or nymph – dressed only in her long hair and a wisp of drapery. In the background was a Pan figure playing reed pipes.

"I shall keep mine in my book of picture cards," said Lucy.

Mary Ann had no such book with her at school. Instead, when they went to their dormitory, she slid her ticket halfway into a crack in the wooden paneling beside her bed.

I'll be able to take it out and remember and be inspired, she thought.

But next day something happened that put all thoughts of Ranelagh and Maria Anna Mozart out of her mind.

CHAPTER SIX

News from Home

It was Saturday morning. The girls were at their first lesson of the day – Arithmetic – when a maid came in and spoke quietly to Mr. Ashton.

"Mary Ann," he said – and she stood up, her heartbeat quickening. "You are to go to Mrs. Neave's office immediately."

She left, catching puzzled glances from her friends, and tapped on Mrs. Neave's door. Surely she'd done nothing wrong?

"Come in!"

Mary Ann opened the door, and was surprised to see her mother sitting opposite Mrs. Neave.

Mrs. Giffard did not look her usual self. Her hands, which she normally held still in her lap, were restless, pulling at the fingers of her gloves.

"Mama?" Mary Ann said uncertainly.

"Don't be alarmed, Mary Ann," said her mother. "No one is ill."

And Mrs. Neave told her, "You are to go home with your mother today. You may return on Monday morning."

"Oh – but…" Mary Ann thought of her singing lesson later that morning: Galatea's song about the dove. She'd been practicing.

"You are excused from your lessons," said Mrs. Neave. "Go and fetch your cloak and shawl and anything else you wish to take with you."

Mary Ann went upstairs. When she came down

again with her outdoor clothes her mother was waiting in the hall.

"Mama, what is it?"

Her mother steered her outside, toward the landing stage on the riverside, before replying.

"The ship – the one your father was expecting: it has sunk."

"Then…he has lost money?" said Mary Ann. She was accustomed to the ups and downs of her father's finances, but they were rarely down for long.

"Yes." Her mother spoke calmly, but there was a tremor in her voice that frightened Mary Ann. "We have lost nearly everything. I had no idea how much he had invested in this, and in another venture which has also failed. We have many creditors. We cannot live as we have been doing. We must economize."

It was a moment before Mary Ann realized the implications of this. Then she said in a voice of rising alarm, "Mama…?"

"You must leave Mrs. Neave's school," her mother

said. She laid a hand on Mary Ann's arm. "Oh, not immediately, dear. You may stay till the end of July, of course; that is paid for. But we can't keep you there for another term."

"July! But there is to be the concert – the school concert – in September. You are to come. And I am to sing in it. And I love being there, Mama, you know that. I can't leave. I can't!"

"Oh, Mary Ann, I'm sorry," her mother said, "but there is simply no money. We'll talk about it at home. Your papa is there, and George is on his way. Look, there's a boat waiting. Compose yourself before we step aboard."

Out on the river and facing toward the City, Mary Ann turned around and watched the shoreline of Chelsea disappearing from view. She felt trapped, helpless. When she looked back at her mother her face was wet with tears.

The boatman pretended not to see. Her mother

said, in a low voice, "We must do as your father thinks best, Mary Ann. You are not the only one to suffer. Think of Harriet – her position now as regards Mr. Browne."

But Mary Ann was too full of her own grief to care about Harriet and her fiancé. All she could think was that this boat was taking her further and further away from where she wanted to be: the house on Chelsea Walk.

CHAPTER SEVEN

"It's Not Fair!"

Mary Ann felt the tension in the house as soon as they arrived home. Even Betty, the kitchen maid, and the manservant Tom looked nervous – as well they might, Mary Ann thought, since they could lose their jobs.

Her father came out of his study to greet her and her mother. He had dark circles under his eyes, and through the half-open door Mary Ann could see papers spread about and a decanter of brandy.

"Well, Kitten!" he said, falsely hearty and using Mary Ann's baby name. "We must tighten our belts for a while. No doubt your mother has told you—"

"Papa!" Mary Ann could not help interrupting. "*Please* don't make me leave school!"

Instead of reprimanding her for her rudeness, her father looked almost apologetic.

"I've no choice, Kitten. Now, now –" he patted her shoulder – "tears won't help." He turned to his wife. "I shall go out to the coffee house; speak to friends. There may be contacts…"

He wants to escape us, Mary Ann thought.

She heard fast footsteps coming downstairs, and George burst into the room.

"Greetings, Little Sister!" He made a long face. "Oh – not you, too! Harriet is all of a mope upstairs, moving her things."

"Moving her things?"

Mrs. Giffard intervened: "I should have told you, Mary Ann. We have made space for you and Harriet in the blue room and will be letting your bedroom and the dressing room to a lodger."

"A lodger! Who?"

They had had financial problems before, but it had never come to this. And the blue room was tiny and overlooked the back yard and the outhouse.

"Do not shout, child. Remember your manners. We shall take a respectable woman. Perhaps even someone who might be able to play or sing a little, and could give you lessons…"

Mary Ann stiffened. She hated the proposed woman already.

"I must go and help Harriet," she said, and turned to the stairs. George followed her up.

Harriet had almost filled the armoire with her gowns. I don't know where mine will go, thought Mary Ann, but she didn't say so because her sister looked so miserable.

"This was not *my* idea," Harriet said defensively.

George crossed the room, leaned on the windowsill

and breathed in, wrinkling his nose. "Better keep this shut when the men come to empty the outhouses," he said.

"It's nothing to joke about, George," retorted Harriet. "*You* don't have to lose your room."

"Mine is smaller still! You would not get two beds in it."

This was true, but George's room was cozier, newly painted in yellow, and with a tiled fireplace. The blue room was shabby; even Amy, the lady's maid, had a fresher one: a small, neat space under the eaves.

"Make yourself useful, George," Harriet pleaded. "Fetch my box of shoes?"

When he had gone out, she turned to Mary Ann: "Father has written to Mr. Browne about my dowry." Her eyes brimmed. "It will be much diminished."

"Oh, Hatty!" For a moment Mary Ann put aside her own troubles. "If Mr. Browne loves you that will make no difference!"

"Have you been reading romances, Mary Ann?

You know love has nothing to do with it. It is my fortune that matters."

"But – he must care for you."

Mary Ann thought dull Mr. Browne should consider himself lucky to have Harriet, who was pretty and well brought up and truly quite amiable most of the time.

"His family will not be in favor of the match now," said Harriet. "Whatever he may feel, they will talk him out of it."

George came in with Harriet's box and placed it on the floor. "You know, Hat, you might have my room most of the year. I'm only home for holidays and vacations."

"You *were*," said Mary Ann. "But now you'll be living at home, won't you?"

There was a silence. Mary Ann looked from George to Harriet, and the truth became plain to her.

"Oh! That's not *fair*!" she cried out.

She flew downstairs. "Mama! *Mama!*"

The parlor was empty. She ran on, down to the basement.

Her mother was in the kitchen, giving instructions to Mrs. Wilson, the cook. She turned a shocked face to her daughter.

"Mama, if George is to stay at school why can't I?"

"Mary Ann, control yourself!"

Her mother took her by the shoulders, her fingers pinching, and steered her out of the kitchen and upstairs to the parlor.

"*Never* let me hear you shouting like that again! And in front of the servants! Has Mrs. Neave taught you nothing?"

"She will not have the chance now!" retorted Mary Ann.

Her mother slapped her face. Mary Ann's eyes watered from the sting and the humiliation. She began to cry in earnest. "It's not fair," she sobbed.

"Of course it is not," her mother said. "When was life ever fair to women? But your father is right.

George's education must prepare him for a career in the City. He will have needs and responsibilities that you will never have. Don't imagine that life is easier for a boy. It is harder, more competitive. Your father would only take George away from that school as a very last resort, if we were penniless. Whereas…"

Whereas my education is unimportant, thought Mary Ann. Even so, she'd fight for it. She said, "I will make a better marriage if I can sing and dance and speak French and behave like a lady."

"A better marriage requires a larger dowry," her mother replied. "I'm sorry, Mary Ann, but there is nothing to be done. We must reduce our expenditure. We intend to sell some of my jewelry—"

"I could sell mine!" Mary Ann interrupted, eager to help.

Her mother brushed the offer aside, as if it was of no consequence. She sighed, and looked around the room, at the new flock wallpaper, the painted floor cover and the long green curtains with their gold tassels: all bought last year.

Mary Ann said tentatively, "We could ask Grandmama Causey."

At once her mother's face closed up. "You know I never approach your grandmother for help."

"But you might…just this once. She might *like* to help."

"I don't doubt she would *like* it," said Mrs. Giffard. "It would give her great satisfaction."

And then she was silent, as if she felt she had said too much. But Mary Ann understood. She knew that for her mother to ask for help now would mean to admit that she had been wrong to marry John Giffard, that he was as unreliable as her parents had said, that they had been right all along.

And she wondered if her mother *did* regret her marriage. Sometimes, in bed at night, she'd heard raised voices, doors slamming; and her father was often away on business.

Marriage was not something that Mary Ann looked

forward to. To become an opera singer – that was her dream. And at Mrs. Neave's she'd felt she was on her way to achieving it.

"If I could have only the singing and harpsichord lessons?" she pleaded. "I don't mind about Geography and Arithmetic, or even Comportment…"

Her mother shook her head.

"Just one more term…the concert—"

"Oh, Mary Ann! Go and talk to Harriet. Don't pester me, *please*!"

They sat on Harriet's bed: Mary Ann, Harriet and George. Mary Ann was going through the contents of her jewelry box. There was a locket – a birthday present from her parents – a child-size silver bracelet, an amber brooch, a necklace of dark red stones.

"Garnets," said Mary Ann.

"Glass," said Harriet. "And you can't sell any of these. Mama would not hear of it."

"If they *were* garnets," said Mary Ann obstinately,

"I might get eight guineas for them."

She remembered from Mrs. Neave's advertisement that the school cost twenty-one guineas a year. Seven guineas would buy her another term there, but she'd need extra for the music lessons.

Harriet took the box from her and closed the lid. "They are glass. And there is nothing any of us can do."

"But it's so unfair! Why should George stay at school and not me?"

"It's a great pity, but you have to see that Father's decision is entirely reasonable," said Harriet.

"And to be expected," agreed George – complacently, Mary Ann thought.

She punched him. "You told me you cared!"

"I *do* care! I'm sorry, truly I am! But I am the son and heir. That's the difference."

On Sunday there was more bad news. A letter came, delivered by a servant, addressed to Harriet. It was from Mr. Philip Browne, who told her that, with great regret, he felt it necessary to break off their engagement. Harriet, weeping, rushed upstairs to the blue bedroom and shut herself in. Her mother followed her. Mary Ann and George, listening nearby, could hear storms of tears from Harriet and soothing noises from their mother. Mr. Giffard kept out of the way in his study.

"She shouldn't waste tears on *him*," said George.

"No," agreed Mary Ann. "He's a toad." "Toad" was Sophia's favorite word for anyone she disliked, and Mary Ann wrinkled her nose, like Sophia, as she said it.

Mr. Browne had made Harriet unhappy, and that was reason enough to dislike him; but what Mary Ann would never have admitted, even to herself, was that she particularly hated Mr. Browne for having focused everyone's attention so exclusively on her older sister. Harriet emerged from her room red-eyed, pale and stricken, unable to eat or to speak above a whisper: the very picture of a jilted bride. Everyone was sorry for her. Later, when Mary Ann once again pleaded to be allowed to stay on at school (for she was to go back there in the morning and this was her last chance) all her mother would say was, "How can you be so selfish? Think of poor Hatty." The whole household, including the servants, was taken up with sympathy for Harriet's cause. No one had time for Mary Ann.

CHAPTER EIGHT

Tea with Mrs. Corelli

Back at school, in the dormitory, it was different. Mary Ann's friends had missed her, and worried about her, and no one knew why she had gone home so suddenly. When she told them her news, they surrounded her with all the sympathy and attention she had longed for at home.

"But that's *terrible!*" exclaimed Sophia.

And even quiet Lucy said, "You *can't* leave us.

There must be something we can do."

They all gathered round and tried to comfort her, and that made Mary Ann cry again.

"Mrs. Neave will help, surely?" said Phoebe.

"No." Mary Ann gulped back tears. She was certain that Mrs. Neave would not help, for how could anyone run a business at a loss?

"I shall talk to Mrs. Corelli," Sophia decided. "*She* won't want to lose you. You're our best singer by far."

"And a good advertisement for the school," Lucy pointed out.

But they all knew Mrs. Corelli was only an employee and could have no say in the matter.

"We're such a friendly little group here," Sophia said – making Mary Ann wail, "I *know!*" and cry even more – "I shall tell Mrs. Corelli that if you leave we might get some *toad* of a girl who can't even *sing*…"

No one had a solution, but their sympathy was comforting, and they even had some left over for

Harriet, though they were not shocked to hear that George would remain at his school.

"That is quite natural, Mary Ann," said Sophia. "Your education cannot be considered as important as your brother's."

"You can't call that unfair," agreed Phoebe.

"You *can*," said Lucy, "but it will not help. It's the way of the world, my mother says."

Everyone at school was kind. Mrs. Neave was especially concerned; and Jenny paused in her work to talk and sympathize.

Mrs. Corelli was determined to look on the bright side.

"You must put all this out of your mind for now, and concentrate on your work," she said. "We have the September concert to prepare for—"

"But I won't be *here* in September!"

Mrs. Corelli shook her head. "Now, Mary Ann, who knows what will happen? Your father's fortunes may have improved by then. We must be ready. And you are my best soprano among the younger girls. Now, what did you intend to sing? An air of Galatea's, wasn't it? And anything else?"

"Yes. Galatea. 'As when the dove…' I like that one. And 'Nymphs and Shepherds'?"

"The choir will sing 'Nymphs and Shepherds.' You'll be part of that." (Mary Ann wished it were true.) "What about 'When Daisies Pied and Violets Blue' for a solo? That's pretty, and would suit your voice. But first, let me hear the Galatea…"

Mary Ann tried hard to think only of the music, to forget her troubles. She sang:

"*As when the dove*
Laments her love
All on the naked spray;
When he returns
No more she mourns
But love the live-long day…"

Her voice broke on "mourns," and spoiled what

should have been the joyful crescendo of the next line. By the end of the song tears were streaming down her cheeks. "I won't be here to sing it!" she wept.

"But you must *learn* it!" insisted Mrs. Corelli. "How else can you be ready when occasion demands? If you are to be a performer, you must always be ready."

"My parents won't allow me to be a singer," said Mary Ann, determined to be sorry for herself.

"Then they are probably wise," Mrs. Corelli said. "It is a difficult choice, the stage, and very few succeed. Oh, Mary Ann! Your voice is quite gone with all this crying. Dry your tears, and come up to my room. I'll make tea."

Mary Ann had always been curious to see inside the teachers' private rooms, and she immediately felt more cheerful as she followed Mrs. Corelli upstairs to the third floor.

Mrs. Corelli's room was across the stairwell from the younger girls' dormitory, and opposite Mrs. Neave's suite. It was a decent size, but filled to overflowing with Mrs. Corelli's possessions. There was a bed, an armoire, a cabinet, a music stand, a table and two chairs, cooking pots and a kettle. And all around the walls and on the mantelpiece and shelves were displayed playbills, engravings, open fans, a plume of feathers, a crimson shawl. The bed was curtained off, but the cooking area by the fireplace was open to the room.

Mrs. Corelli put the kettle on a trivet over the fire, then took a small key from a bag at her waist and unlocked a little black lacquered tea caddy. Mary Ann felt privileged to be given tea, which was so expensive.

"It's cozy here. I like it," she said, watching Mrs. Corelli measure a spoonful of tea into the warmed pot.

"But hardly what *you* are accustomed to?"

"Well…until Hatty and I were put together, I had a bedroom all to myself…"

"In a big house, with servants to wait on you?"

"Yes."

"I might have had the same, if I had not followed my heart."

Mary Ann had already noticed, in a frame on the wall opposite, a small painting of a young man, dark and slightly foreign-looking.

"Is that Mr. Corelli?" she asked.

"Yes." Mrs. Corelli placed two cups of tea on the table. The cups were cracked but pretty. Mary Ann's had medallions painted on it enclosing scenes of cupids and goddesses.

"My husband was a singer," Mrs. Corelli explained. "Italian. He had a fine voice and was much sought after by the opera companies."

"He was famous?" Mary Ann was entranced. "How did you meet? Where?" In her excitement she quite forgot to be deferential to her teacher.

Mrs. Corelli did not seem to mind the informality. "At Drury Lane Theater," she said. "I was a singer too."

"Oh! I knew it!" exclaimed Mary Ann. Mrs. Corelli

was no longer young, but she moved like an actress and her clothes were always a little more flamboyant than you'd expect in a teacher. ("She knows how to wear a shawl," Sophia had said once.) "Were *you* famous?"

"A little, for a while."

She opened a drawer and brought out a green cloth-covered box. Inside were old tickets, advertisements, playbills, prints of engravings.

"Here is all my life, and my husband's, on the stage."

Mary Ann leafed through them: "…*The Beggars' Opera*…the part of MacHeath played by Enrico Corelli" … "Enrico and Jane Corelli" … "the celebrated Mr. Corelli…" … "Mrs. Corelli excels as Margarita…"

"Oh! This is wonderful!" She sighed. "I wish I might do the same!"

"It did not last long," said Mrs. Corelli. "We had some good years. But now, you see, I am a widow, and my voice and looks are not what they were, and my home is this little room…"

"I *love* your room!"

Mrs. Corelli laughed. "So do I, my dear! It's my haven. But you know, the stage is a difficult life without much reward for most people. And to achieve even a small success you must work hard, and practice daily, and above all be ready! Never give up hope."

A bell rang far below, and she stood up. "We shall practice again on Wednesday, and you will be in good voice and dry-eyed. Is that agreed?"

"Yes, Mrs. Corelli."

She went out. The bell meant it was time for the afternoon break, and the girls would be gathering in the dining room for lemonade. Well, she didn't need any; she'd had tea! She went into the dormitory and sat on her bed and pulled out the Ranelagh ticket from its crack in the paneling. She gazed at the nymph in her swirling drapery and Pan playing his pipes, and imagined just such a ticket announcing her own appearance as the nymph Galatea.

Mrs. Corelli had cheered her up and made her feel

that anything was possible. She saw now that she needed to work to make her own fortune. If her parents could not pay, she must find the money for next term herself in the only way she knew: she must sing for the money.

CHAPTER NINE

Plans

"I guessed, the first time I saw her!" declared Sophia, when Mary Ann told the other three about Mrs. Corelli having been on the stage. "I said so to you, did I not, Lucy? I said, 'You can see from the way she moves that she is an actress.'"

"But you haven't been inside her room," said Phoebe enviously. "You haven't seen the portrait of Mr. Corelli."

"No… We must find a way to be invited, all of us."

"Lose our voices?" joked Lucy.

They laughed. But they were jealous. Mary Ann knew it was not a good time to share with them her idea of singing to raise money for her fees. She had thought, at first, about a concert organized by the four of them, but she soon foresaw the difficulty of finding either an audience who would pay or a place to stage it. Even if it were allowed, it would be humiliating to perform at school and let everyone know that her parents could not afford the fees. She realized that she needed to do this by herself. She remembered the ballad singers she always liked to hear in the streets of London. Those women would have a hat on the ground, or an assistant who went in amongst the crowd asking for money. They must do well on market days.

But ballad singing was unthinkable. She was a merchant's daughter. She could not stand in the street and sing.

It was the next day, when she glanced out of the window during a Geography lesson, and saw Jenny hanging out washing in the garden, that the answer came to her. Surely Jenny would help! She sang in a tavern; she'd even sung at Ranelagh, with her cousin.

She waited until the next time she saw Jenny going into the laundry room alone, then followed her in and closed the door.

"Oh, Miss!" Jenny turned round. "You startled me!"

She'd had a slightly guilty manner ever since the affair of the pillowcases.

Mary Ann spoke quietly. "Jenny, I need your help. Will you be singing – performing – again soon?"

"Oh, yes, Miss!" Jenny's face cleared. "I'm going with my cousin to Ranelagh a week from Saturday."

"To Ranelagh!" This was even better than Mary Ann could have hoped. Surely at Ranelagh, among so many wealthy people, she would earn enough money to keep her here at least one more term?

"It's a masquerade night," Jenny explained. "Everyone will be masked, even the people working the booths."

"Masks!" Mary Ann was enthralled. "Will *you* wear a mask?"

"Oh, yes – to blend in! It should be a good night: dancing and all sorts of entertainments going on till the small hours of the morning."

"Take me with you!" Mary Ann begged. "Let me sing too!"

"*You*, Miss?" Jenny looked horrified. "Oh – I couldn't – no, not you. It's not suitable… I'd be in trouble. And Nick, my cousin – he'd never agree."

"Please, Jenny, *please*! You know why. I need eight guineas for next term. There's no other way for me to earn it."

"You'd never get eight guineas, Miss."

"But I'd get something! It would be a start. And it would be secret. The masks. We'd be disguised." It seemed a chance she could not forgo.

"No." Jenny's face was set. "No, I daren't do it. I'm sorry."

"I helped *you*," Mary Ann said. "I never told anyone what I saw. Those pillowcases…"

She hated herself even as she spoke. It was wrong: blackmail. But it worked. Jenny looked wary.

"I'll ask Nick," she said. "I'll see him on Sunday. "But it'll be up to him, Miss, and I reckon he'll say no. Indeed, I'm sure he will."

Mary Ann waited. She was in a fever of impatience for the rest of the week, and could not attend to her lessons or to the gossip of her friends. But when she went for her next singing lesson with Mrs. Corelli she managed to put her anxiety aside and worked hard at the songs. These were important. Mrs. Corelli had told her that she must be ready at all times, and she was determined she would be: ready for Ranelagh. Mrs. Corelli was surprised and pleased, and praised her.

On Sunday Mary Ann was restless, biting her nails

in church, wondering when Jenny would be back and when the two of them would have a chance to talk.

At last, when they were going in to supper, she caught a glimpse of Jenny in the back part of the house. Jenny saw her, and flicked a glance upwards, and Mary Ann broke from her friends, saying, "I forgot my handkerchief!" and darted upstairs.

Jenny, meanwhile, had hurried up the back stairs.

They met on the second floor landing, near the linen-storage room.

Jenny was breathless. "He says – yes!"

"Oh!" Mary Ann was so pleased that she flung her arms around the maid and hugged her.

Jenny seemed rather less delighted. "Fool that I am, I told him what a sweet voice you had, and he says the folks there will love it, a young one like you singing. But we need to get you out, and back again, without Mrs. Neave's knowing. And that won't be easy."

Mary Ann hadn't even thought about the mechanics of her plan; gaining Jenny's agreement to it had been what obsessed her. Now she realized that she would be breaking the school rules by going out unauthorized and at night. She could be in serious trouble if Mrs. Neave found out – expelled, even. But then she had nothing to lose. Unlike Jenny.

"You must not tell your friends," said Jenny. "If you give even a hint to those tattletales, we're finished. Do you understand? Promise?"

"I promise. Thank you, Jenny."

It would be a long week, she thought, keeping such a secret to herself.

CHAPTER TEN

Out at Night

It was Saturday morning – the day of the masquerade at Ranelagh Gardens.

"We'll go to Ranelagh after dark," said Jenny. She was folding sheets in the linen room, with an eye open for Mrs. Price, whose voice could be heard downstairs. "About half past ten."

"So late!" Mary Ann was always in bed by nine.

"Oh, people will arrive late," said Jenny, "and stay

till morning. These grand folk keep strange hours!" She lowered her voice still further. "Can you slip out without the other girls seeing?"

"I think so."

"Don't let them in on this. I'm risking my place. You know that."

"Yes."

"Come down the back stairs and I'll be waiting. I'll make some excuse to stay late in the kitchen. The doors will be locked, but there's a window we can climb through."

A window! Mary Ann felt nervous. She'd never done anything like this before, but Jenny spoke as if climbing out of a window was an everyday occurrence. She nodded.

"I'll bring a mask for you. Wear something pretty."

"My best dress!"

"No, not that! But a bright color. You've got a rosy pink one, haven't you? And have some lace and ribbons about you. But don't wear a hoop under your skirt. And you'll need sturdy shoes – not those." She glanced down at Mary Ann's light-soled fabric slippers.

Mrs. Price appeared at the top of the stairs. "Jenny, are you –" She stopped in surprise at the sight of Mary Ann. "The young ladies are all at their lessons, Miss."

"I – lost a book..." Mary Ann said, and darted away downstairs, terrified that their plan would be discovered. She slipped into Mrs. Neave's English lesson with a curtsy and downcast eyes, murmuring a similar apology, and receiving a reprimand.

"What are you up to?" Sophia demanded afterward. "I saw you with Jenny. You keep chatting with her."

"No, I don't!" Mary Ann's heart hammered. "Well, not often. But she's my friend; you know that. She's kind."

To distract the others, she suggested a visit to the Bun House that afternoon. There were always teachers or older pupils willing to supervise a Saturday outing there. On the way they stopped at a haberdasher's, and Mary Ann bought some pink ribbon for her hair.

Later, after supper, she made an excuse of tidying the gowns hanging in the armoire, and put her rose-sprigged cotton gown within easy reach, with a fringed shawl draped over it. She placed her shoes, with stockings rolled inside them, where she could find them in the dark. The armoire door squeaked when you opened it, so she left it ajar and hoped no one else would close it.

The girls sat about in their nightgowns and combed their hair and talked about their day. They reminisced happily about the sugary buns they'd bought and the array of ribbons and lace at the haberdasher's. Mary Ann was quiet, but hoped the others would put it down to her unhappiness at the thought of leaving them all. If only she could tell them! But she'd promised Jenny, and probably it was safer this way.

"Let me comb your hair, Mary Ann!" Sophia begged; and Mary Ann agreed, and let Sophia twist it into curls and tie the new pink ribbons in it. She planned to leave them in at bedtime, as if by accident.

The clock on the second floor landing had just struck nine when Mrs. Neave put her head around the door and said, "Into bed now, girls."

"Oh, Mrs. Neave, it's still light outside!" protested Sophia.

"Then draw the curtains, child. You don't want to be tired for church tomorrow."

She went out, closing the door, and Sophia giggled and said, "I might as well be. I always sleep through the sermon."

"*So* dull!" agreed Phoebe.

But they allowed Mary Ann, who was nearest the window, to draw the curtains, and all wished each other goodnight and got into bed.

Mary Ann lay waiting. Sophia fell asleep quickly, as she usually did; her breathing soon became slow and steady. Then came the little snuffling sounds that Phoebe always made in her sleep. Lucy was quiet. But she was on the other side of the room, near the door, and Mary Ann knew she was a light sleeper.

She dared not move too soon.

She heard the clock strike ten. Was Jenny downstairs, in the kitchen? Probably all the servants were still there. She lay wide awake, waiting a while longer, to give the maids and teachers time to go upstairs to their rooms. She heard creakings, low voices; but at last the house seemed to be still, full of a soft breathing quiet.

She slid out of bed, went to the armoire, and glanced at Lucy: dark hair on the pillow, face turned away. She took her gown off its hook, picked up her shoes, then opened the door. It made a faint click. When she looked back, Lucy had turned over, but she seemed to be asleep. Mary Ann crept out, closing the door softly behind her, and padded barefoot across the landing to the back stairs.

The stairs were pitch dark. She felt her way down a few steps, then stopped and put on her stockings and shoes. She slipped the dress on over her nightbown and draped the shawl around her shoulders. The dress had a boned bodice and did not require stays, but she'd need Jenny's help to do it up.

The stairs creaked alarmingly as she moved down: one, two, three flights. And at the bottom there was a cold stone floor underfoot, and a chilly draft. She'd never been in the basement before. This was where the kitchen staff spent nearly all their time.

There was a door to her right, half open. She touched it, and heard Jenny's voice: "Who's there?"

"It's me: Mary Ann."

"Ah." Jenny sounded relieved.

Next moment a candle came alight, and Mary Ann saw the gleam of eyes. Jenny looked beautiful in a red dress, low cut, her dark hair in curls under a little tilted hat with a gray feather.

"Are you ready?" she asked.

"Yes. But can you help me do up my dress?"

She felt Jenny's hands at her back. "There." Jenny tied the shawl securely in place over it. "You'll need your hands free. What a fine pair we are!" She glanced at the window. "My cousin will be waiting – if you're sure you want to come?"

"Yes. Yes, of course!"

"Right." Jenny led her to the scullery window. There was a shallow stone sink under it, and a wooden table at the side. They hitched up their skirts and climbed onto the table. Then Jenny blew out the candle and Mary Ann felt her move away, into the sink, and heard the sound of the sash window being cautiously raised. Cool air flowed in.

"Follow me. And try not to make a sound climbing out. Mrs. Price's window is just above."

Mary Ann could see enough to know that Jenny was out through the window and down on the pavement outside. She'd moved quickly, despite her full skirts, and Mary Ann realized it wasn't the first time she'd gone out this way. She struggled to follow: found her footing on the edge of the sink, turned, and went out backward, Jenny's hands on her waist guiding her down.

Jenny pulled the window back into place, took Mary Ann's hand, and ran with her up the basement steps, then down the length of the dark garden, keeping close to the wall. She unlatched the tradesmen's gate at the end, and they both slipped out onto Robinson's Lane.

A man was waiting in the shadows.

"Nick!" Jenny drew Mary Ann around to face him. "Here's our young lady: Mary Ann."

Nick was slim and tall, like Jenny. He wore a yellow spotted kerchief around his neck and a black hat and carried a violin case on a strap across his body. He made a hint of a bow to Mary Ann, then said, "Let's find a boat."

They went to the waterfront, where the pier was thronging with people – to Mary Ann's surprise, for the hour seemed late to her.

Soon they were in a boat, being rowed across the dark water. Mary Ann shivered, despite her shawl. It was not such a fine evening as on her last visit, and there were spots of rain on the wind. But she grew warmer with anticipation as they came within sight of Ranelagh and saw the gardens lit with thousands of lanterns, the white Temple of Pan gleaming from a distance, and lights all along the waterfront reflected and moving on the river, like stars. She heard music and, as they arrived at the pier, a busy hum of voices. People, some already masked, swept past, wafting perfume.

She had assumed that Nick and Jenny had tickets or performers' passes, and that they would all go in through the same gate as everyone else, but the two of them led her away from the gate, along a path that wound around the perimeter of the gardens, which were bordered by a fence and a high hedge.

There were fewer lights here, and it was muddy. She caught Jenny's hand. "Where are we going?"

"Ssh! Nick knows the way."

They stopped, and Mary Ann saw a break in the fence: a picket missing. Jenny at once squeezed through and, with a bit of rustling and a soft curse, disappeared from sight.

It was then that Mary Ann realized, all in a rush, that Nick and Jenny were not licensed to perform at the gardens, as she'd supposed; that they were breaking in; that they'd done this before; and that they could all end up in much worse trouble than she'd risked already by leaving school without permission.

"I don't think –" she began. But Nick said, "You next, Miss," and pushed her ahead of him through the gap. She felt the prickly branches of the hedge on her face and arms, and heard Jenny whisper, "There's a way through here. Bit of a squeeze. Mind yourself on the thorns."

Nick was behind her, and Jenny caught her from in front, and together they helped her through. No wonder Jenny had told her not to wear her best dress, Mary Ann thought.

They emerged onto a dark path among trees, faintly lit by lights further along.

Nick stood up, adjusted his hat, and said, "Welcome to Ranelagh, ladies. Shall we find ourselves a spot?"

CHAPTER ELEVEN

Masquerade

He took their arms, one on each side of him, and Mary Ann thought: a man has offered me his arm! How jealous Sophia would be! And she felt suddenly grownup and grateful to Mrs. Corelli for the comportment lessons.

Now that they were inside the gardens, unchallenged, she began to feel less anxious. Nick and Jenny seemed quite carefree, chatting as they walked along the path.

Nick struck out confidently toward the lights and movement, and occasionally they passed groups of young men, or couples who whispered and laughed together. Most of them were masked. Some way off Mary Ann could see the Temple of Pan, where a constant movement of people flowed to and fro. Closer to hand, there were other attractions: a juggler, people in costume: a man dressed as Punch, a woman in harem trousers and a flimsy top that shocked Mary Ann. All around were little booths with lanterns hanging outside, the candle flames flickering in the breeze. These sold candy and drinks.

Nick stopped by a natural arbor at the side of the path, where a lantern swung in the branches, and let go of the girls' arms. "This will do," he said. He opened the violin case and took out the instrument, and placed his hat on the ground.

Jenny produced masks: a black and gilt one for Nick, sparkling green for herself, and blue and silver for Mary Ann. Once her mask was tied in place

Mary Ann felt safer. No one would know her now.

Nick began to play: a sweet, romantic tune. And he looked the part, with his dramatic pose, the fiddle on his shoulder, the yellow kerchief catching the light.

Jenny took Mary Ann to a stall and bought her a bag of sugared almonds. She also asked for two glasses of wine, and one of lemondade for Mary Ann. "That'll wet your whistle," she said.

Mary Ann sipped the lemonade as they walked back.

A few people had paused to listen to Nick's playing. Mary Ann heard a chinking of coins in the hat. Nick called to Jenny, "A song, sweetheart!" He began to play an air from *The Beggars' Opera* that Mary Ann knew; and Jenny stood beside him and sang, holding out her arms in dramatic gestures like the ladies at the opera and drawing cries of admiration from the gathering crowd. The gentlemen, who all seemed to walk around in noisy groups, cheered and threw coins as the song ended. Jenny smiled and curtsied, the red dress sweeping the ground, her dark eyes shining.

"Encore!" someone – drunk, by the sound of him – shouted. But Jenny turned to Mary Ann and drew her forward. "Sing that dove song," she whispered. "Tell Nick; he'll know it…"

Nick did know it, and began to play Galatea's air, and Mary Ann sang – too softly at first to be heard over the wind and rustling leaves and drunken chatter of passers-by. But then a hush fell, and people listened, and her voice soared clear:

"As when the dove
Laments her love,
All on the naked spray;
When he returns,
No more she mourns,
But love the live-long day…"

At the end, as she curtsied, loud clapping broke out, and Mary Ann heard women's voices: "Such a sweet child!" "Another Miss Mozart, I do believe!"

They called for more – and Nick caught her eye and began to play the tune again.

The hat was filling nicely. When the crowd moved on, Jenny scooped up most of the contents and stowed it away in a pocket hidden beneath a slit in her skirt. Nick laid down the fiddle and put an arm around each of them.

"You were right, Jenny!" he said. "She sings like an angel. And *I* was right to tell you to bring her. The ladies love it!" He turned to Mary Ann. "What else do you know, sweetheart? Could you sing a duet with Jenny?"

They sang a few more songs – Mary Ann joining Jenny in familiar ballads, then one or other of them singing alone. Nick encouraged Mary Ann to sing her "operatic stuff" as he called it. "They like that." But when she tried to copy Jenny's extravagant gestures he shook his head at her. "Keep it sweet and simple," he said afterward. "Suits you better."

And the people enjoyed it. The hat began to fill again, and once more Jenny transferred its contents to her pocket. Mary Ann sipped her lemonade and nibbled her sugared almonds between songs as the night grew cool. Although it was drizzling, more and more people were strolling along the paths: groups of loud-voiced young men, or couples arm-in-arm.

When she was not singing, Mary Ann listened to snatches of conversation. She heard women talk of a lighted gondola on the canal, and of a row of little shops selling fans and other finery; and she could hear, from a distance, sounds of an orchestra playing dance music. She turned wistfully in its direction. She was glad her singing was appreciated, and that Nick was pleased with her, and especially glad to see the money dropping into the hat, but it seemed that much more was happening in the main part of the gardens, nearer the Rotunda, and she wished that they could go there. She wanted to see the Chinese bridge all lit up, and the gondola, and the dancers in their elaborate masks. But Jenny said no, they must stay here, and Mary Ann guessed it was because they had broken in and must keep away from any officials. It was so different from her last visit, and she felt disappointed.

Despite the cool weather the crowds did not lessen, and the revelers were becoming noisier and more drunken. Gangs of men lurched by, and Mary Ann felt afraid when they stared at Jenny in her red dress and shouted coarse remarks. She was sure that only the presence of Nick kept them safe. A fight broke out just ahead of them on the path, and a man, supported by his friends, was left with blood running down his face onto his shirt. Further off, where the lamps petered out and little winding paths led in among dark trees, they heard occasional shrieks and scuffles, and once a young woman burst out and rushed past them, sobbing.

"We should go now," said Jenny, and Nick agreed. He bent to pick up the violin case – and at that moment two men sprang out of the darkness. Mary Ann saw one of them leap on Nick, and then the other pushed her to the ground. She landed hard, the breath knocked from her body, and hit her hand on something sharp. When she looked up, she saw Jenny grappling with the man, screeching, "Thief!" But he flung her down and scooped up the contents of the hat and was gone, in among the trees.

Jenny and Mary Ann both stood up. Nick's attacker had punched him to the ground and fled. He struggled up, cursing.

"Oh, Mary Ann – Miss! Are you hurt?" Jenny looked panic-stricken at the sight of her.

"No…only my hand – I may have cut it…" Mary Ann was trembling, on the brink of tears. "The money?" she said.

"Gone. But don't fret. It wasn't much. Most of it's here –" She patted her hidden pocket.

She turned to Nick, who had a split lip but seemed otherwise unhurt. "Let's get out of here," she said, "before there's any more trouble."

They hurried back along the path toward the place where they had come in. Mary Ann was crying now, from shock and fear. They passed several groups of people, but although Jenny looked disheveled and Nick had a bloody face, no one asked if they needed help. The gardens had become a frightening place. Nick and Jenny hurried her along, and when Nick found the right spot they bundled her quickly through the hedge with its sharp thorns and then out through the gap in the fence onto the path by the river.

It was raining harder now, and Mary Ann was cold; her hand hurt and her face and arms smarted from scratches. The few people they passed on the path looked either drunk or threatening, and she was glad when they reached the dock and found boatmen still available for hire. What time was it? she wondered. Surely it must be the middle of the night? People were leaving Ranelagh, parties of them coming through the gate, but there were still many more inside.

They climbed into a boat. The boatman looked them over suspiciously and said, "Bit of a scrap, eh?" And Mary Ann saw, in the light of his lantern, that her dress was muddied all down the front and her hands were dirty and one was bleeding. She whispered to Jenny, "How will I get clean? I can't go to my bed like this…"

Jenny looked at her and frowned, biting her lip. "No. We need to wash those cuts and tidy you up first. Don't worry. We can use the kitchen sink."

But she looked shaken, and Mary Ann knew that she was worried.

CHAPTER TWELVE

Gin with Mrs. Bolt

They divided up the takings on the waterfront. Mary Ann's share was more than three guineas. She stowed the coins away in her pocket, and would have felt pleased if she had not been so anxious. It had all gone so well until they were attacked, but now…

They parted from Nick, who slipped away down a narrow street and disappeared. The school was close, but Jenny hesitated. "We need to clean you up, but we could be caught if we do it in the kitchen: the noise of water, and the delay... Come to my ma's place. It's just along there, see –" she pointed along the waterfront – "by the Half Moon. We can wash there, and then go back to the school. Safer that way."

Mary Ann followed her obediently. She was relying on Jenny now.

The cottage was tiny – and Jenny's mother only rented the first floor room. As they approached the door Jenny murmured, "With luck she'll have passed out."

Mary Ann was puzzled by this remark until they went in and she saw a large, disheveled woman sprawled in a chair by the fireside, breathing heavily. The woman woke with a snort, turned and glared at Jenny.

"What are *you* doing here? Where have you been, dressed like that?"

"I've been to Ranelagh with Nick," Jenny said, in a hard voice that Mary Ann had not heard from her before. "Not that it's any business of yours."

The woman struggled unsteadily to her feet, and her eyes narrowed in her fleshy face. "Who's this you've brought?"

A nearby curtain twitched open a crack, revealing a bed which seemed to contain several children. Two of them began coughing as they woke up. A young voice asked, "Have you brought anything for us, Jenny?"

"Now you've woken the brats," the woman said; and, to the inhabitants of the bed, "Shut that curtain! And your noise!"

Mary Ann felt frightened and out of place. The room was lit by a single tallow candle, which stank of animal fat. Damp laundry hung in every available space: around the fire, on racks from the ceiling. Was it all their own, she wondered, or did Jenny's mother take in washing? On a table was an end of a loaf, and on the floor by the woman's feet an empty bottle – gin, Mary Ann supposed.

A slight sound from the shadows by the hearth

drew her attention. A smaller bed had been placed there, open to the warmth of the fire, and she saw a pale face and tangled brown hair on the pillow.

Jenny dropped to her knees beside the bed. "Dinah, my pet," she said – and her voice now was soft and concerned. "How are you? Poorly?" She looked up. "Ma, have you been giving her that cordial I bought from Mr. Green?"

"Course I did. And made broth, but she won't take it, hardly any. Betty sat with her, spooning it." A watery look came into her eyes. "She's going, Jenny. She's going fast."

"Ssh! She'll hear!" Jenny stroked Dinah's hair. This must be the sister who was ill, Mary Ann realized. "It's all right, Dinah. Jenny's here."

The girl drifted back to sleep.

"She smells," said Jenny, reverting to her hard, accusing voice. "You ought to change her linen."

"Can't do everything, can I?" The woman frowned again at Mary Ann. "Who's she?"

Jenny stood up and put an arm around Mary Ann's shoulders, and drew her forward. "One of the young ladies from the school." And she added sarcastically to Mary Ann: "My mother, Mrs. Bolt."

"What's she doing here?" Mrs. Bolt demanded.

But Jenny ignored her, lit another candle, and took Mary Ann out to a back room, where she filled a jug with water from a pail. Part of the main room had been partitioned off with a curtain. Jenny drew the curtain aside and led Mary Ann in. A bed took up most of the space. Next to it was a tiny washstand and a few inches of floor.

"This is *my* space – private," said Jenny. "Any of them comes in here, they get my fist."

Jenny's bed was neat and fresh – a miracle in that house, Mary Ann thought. Her clothes hung on pegs, and the washstand was clean.

She poured water into the bowl. "I'm sorry it's cold, but we can't stop to heat it. Here –" She took a cloth, wetted it and wiped Mary Ann's face, hands and arms in a way that made Mary Ann think she'd done this often, for younger brothers and sisters. The cut hand stung, and blood flowed into the water. Jenny washed it thoroughly, then tore a strip of cloth from something to make a bandage. "You can take that off in the morning. 'Tisn't as bad as it looks. Now, that dress…"

With a dry cloth she brushed at the mud as best she could. "It needs proper cleaning. I'll try and do it with the school wash. Your shoes are not too bad. But your hair…" She took the ribbons out and began combing Mary Ann's hair.

"Ouch!"

"It's all tangled with bits of twig," said Jenny. "Got to get them out. There!" She surveyed Mary Ann. "You don't look so bad now." And as she began to tidy herself, she asked, "Pleased with your money, are you?"

"Yes."

"They liked your singing. I reckon Nick would

be happy to have you with him again!" She put a hand to her pocket. "I'll be able to get some proper medicine for Dinah."

Mary Ann felt troubled. She had never been in a house where people were so poor. Whatever Mrs. Bolt did for a living it seemed that she regularly got drunk and that they all relied on Jenny. It made her own anxiety to continue her singing, comportment and dancing lessons seem frivolous – like icing on a cake: delightful, perhaps, but hardly necessary. These were people who truly needed a few extra guineas. She reached into her own pocket and took out her money, all of it, and held it out to Jenny. "You have it, Jenny. Use it for Dinah, or the other little ones."

"What? Don't be silly." Jenny pushed her hand away.

"But you need it more than I do."

"Keep your money," said Jenny. "You earned it. Come on now. I have to get you home."

Getting back into the school was not as easy as climbing out. Jenny found a flowerpot, and used that to stand on and swing herself up to the sill, where she crouched and slid open the window. The pot scraped against the ground as Mary Ann followed, and they both froze, willing Mrs. Price not to have heard them. Once inside, Mary Ann felt safer. But they had still to creep upstairs in total darkness.

The first floor was the easiest: only Mrs. Price slept on that floor, and she was on the other side of the house. But on the second floor were the dormitories, one of them close to the back stairs. Mary Ann's heart beat fast every time a stair creaked. But no one stirred, and they set off more confidently for the third floor, feeling their way up. They were almost at the top when Jenny stumbled and slipped down onto the step below with a bump and a muttered curse. Mary Ann thought she would die of fright. Mrs. Corelli's room was next to the stairwell. They waited. Had she heard anything? There was no sound from within.

Now they had reached the landing. Jenny had one more flight to go, up to the attic. Mary Ann had reached her own floor, but she must pass both Mrs. Neave's and Mrs. Corelli's doors before she reached the dormitory.

Jenny gave her a little push. "Go on," she whispered. "I'll wait and make sure you're safe."

They moved apart – and at that moment Mary Ann heard a door open. She gasped as a light appeared in the corridor: a candle, held up in a trembling hand to reveal the startled face of Mrs. Corelli under her nightcap.

"Who…?" she quavered; then, "Mary Ann! Jenny! Whatever is going on?"

CHAPTER THIRTEEN

Caught!

Doors opened all around: Mrs. Neave's, the dormitory; there were even footsteps and voices on the attic landing above.

Then Mrs. Neave emerged, carrying a candle in a holder and wrapped in a dark-colored robe. Lucy stood blinking and astonished at the end of the corridor.

"Go back to bed, Lucy," said Mrs. Neave. "At once!"

Lucy vanished, pulling the dormitory door shut behind her. Mary Ann longed to be there, safe in the dormitory with Lucy and the others. But she was caught; she could not escape now.

Jenny began to gabble: "Young Miss was taken poorly. I heard her call, and came down. She's better now…" And she edged Mary Ann toward the dormitory, away from the accusing light of the candles.

But Mrs. Neave caught Mary Ann by the shoulder and swung her around. "You have been *outside*!" she said.

Mary Ann knew there was no denying it: her dirty shoes and the mud all down her gown gave her away. Mrs. Neave raised the candle higher and looked at Jenny, who was backing toward the stairs: Jenny with her red dress and white neck and her hat with its jaunty feather. Jenny could hardly pretend she had come down from her bed to attend to a sick girl.

Mrs. Neave's voice was cold: "Go to your room,

Jenny, and report to me first thing in the morning, in my office."

Mary Ann began, "Mrs. Neave, don't blame—"

"As for you, Mary Ann, you will come downstairs now and explain yourself."

Mary Ann reached out wordlessly to Jenny as the maid turned to go. Don't leave me, she wanted to say. She was terrified at the thought of being interrogated alone. But Mrs. Neave gripped her by the shoulders and propelled her toward the stairs. Mary Ann knew from that grip that she was furious.

"I should be grateful if you would come too, Mrs. Corelli," said Mrs. Neave.

As they began to descend Mary Ann heard the dormitory door click open again and voices whispering. Her friends. How she wished she was with them! She felt tears welling up.

She was taken to Mrs. Neave's office. If she had not been so frightened she might have seen the ludicrous side of the situation: the two ladies in nightcaps and robes facing her as inquisitors in the middle of the night. Mrs. Neave positioned herself behind her desk, but Mrs. Corelli, who had come down barefoot, sat to one side swathed in a lavender-colored robe and with her hair – or as much of it as was showing – in curl papers. Mary Ann herself was obliged to stand alone in the middle of the floor. Her tears had spilled over on the way downstairs and now great sobs shook her. When Mrs. Neave demanded an explanation she was unable to speak.

"Calm yourself," said Mrs. Neave – to no effect. Her frosty tone only made Mary Ann cry more. Mrs. Corelli suggested, "Perhaps a glass of water...?" and was permitted to fetch one from the decanter on the sideboard.

Mrs. Neave began a bombardment of questions: "Where have you been? Why? What *can* you have been doing? And how did you get so dirty?"

Mary Ann's teeth clunked against the glass and tears rolled down her cheeks as she tried to explain about her plan to raise the money for her school fees.

"*Ranelagh?*" exclaimed Mrs. Neave. "Jenny took you to *Ranelagh* – on a masquerade night? How could the girl possibly afford tickets?"

"We…we broke in. Through a hole in the fence…" Mary Ann saw Mrs. Neave's eyes widening in horror, but she could think of nothing else to tell except the truth. She was forced to explain how they had gotten out of school through the scullery window, how they had been attacked and robbed, how she had fallen; and all the time she knew she was betraying Jenny, who hadn't wanted to do this at all.

"Please don't blame Jenny!" she said. "I made her do it. I – talked her into it…" She'd been about to say "blackmailed" but that would have meant more betrayal, and she checked herself just in time. "If it wasn't for me," she said, smearing tears across her face with the back of her hand, "Jenny wouldn't have needed to come back here at all. She could have gone home, to her mother's. Sunday's her day off."

"Jenny may be free to go home," said Mrs. Neave coldly, "but she is not free to break out of this house and leave a window unlocked – and especially –" her voice rose – "to take one of my charges with her!" She turned on Mary Ann. "Imagine if something worse had happened to you! If the police had been called? What would I have told your parents? Think of the school's reputation! How many people saw you at Ranelagh?"

"I don't know…a lot…"

"A large number of people who may have guessed where you came from!"

"They only spoke of my singing," said Mary Ann, adding, "Some – several – of them…I don't think they'd remember. They were drunk."

"Drunk!" Mrs. Neave stood up. "And you were there, at night, performing to drunken people…" She turned to Mrs. Corelli: "You know what these masquerade evenings are like. If this becomes known we could be closed down."

Mary Ann began to cry harder than ever. "I'm sorry.

I'm so sorry…" And Mrs. Corelli got up and patted her and gave her a handkerchief and said, "I think Mary Ann should go to bed now, Mrs. Neave."

Mrs. Neave herself seemed suddenly to crumple and look weary. "Yes, indeed, you're right." She turned to Mary Ann and said brusquely, "Dry your eyes, child. At least you've come to no harm. And if you have any money in your pocket you had better give it to me for safekeeping."

Mary Ann untied her pocket and handed it to Mrs. Neave.

She had been crying for so long that she had a lump of pain in her chest that caught at her with every breath. "I wanted – I only wanted – to earn some money," she said, the words coming out in gasps. "Eight guineas. For next term. I don't want to leave."

The two teachers exchanged a glance, and Mrs. Neave said, more kindly, "I understand. But it is not in your power to raise that money, Mary Ann. Nor in mine. Now go to bed. You may sleep in the sick room tonight. I don't want you disturbing the other girls. Mrs. Corelli will take you up."

The sick room was an annex attached to Mrs. Neave's suite of rooms by a connecting door. It contained a narrow bed and a washstand and looked, Mary Ann thought, like a prison cell.

Mrs. Corelli saw her look, and seemed to guess what she was thinking. She gave Mary Ann a hug. "Don't worry. It won't seem so bad in the morning. Go to sleep now."

She shut the door, and Mary Ann lay down alone in the little room and cried with her fist pushed hard against her mouth. It wasn't only her own disgrace that distressed her; it was knowing that she'd brought trouble on Jenny. She couldn't forgive herself for that.

Soon she heard the first birds chirping outside. There was a pale, cold light in the room.

I'll never sleep, she thought. But she did.

She woke late. There was no sound from the other side of the connecting door. She got out of bed and, still in her nightgown, cautiously opened the door to the corridor. Smells and sounds of breakfast rose from below: a distant clatter of cutlery, a hum of voices.

Breakfast. That meant it was at least half past seven. The maids would have been up for hours. And Mrs. Neave had told Jenny to report to her first thing.

With a sense of foreboding, Mary Ann darted barefoot out of the room and upstairs to the attic.

"Jenny…?"

She'd never been up here before and didn't know which room Jenny slept in. She pushed tentatively at a door. It opened to reveal a long, low-ceilinged room containing three beds. Two were made up. One had been stripped.

"Jenny!"

She ran out, and collided with a maid coming in: Ellen, the kitchen maid, a skinny girl with a hunted expression – always in trouble.

"Oh, Miss! You scared me!" She looked hangdog. "Been sent to change my apron."

The apron was filthy with hand-wipings. Mary Ann shuddered. "Where's Jenny?" she asked. "Is she downstairs?"

"She's gone!" The girl's eyes lit up at the prospect of gossip.

"Gone?"

"Yes! Got her wages, packed, and left. Been dismissed!"

"But she can't –"

Mary Ann ran to the dormitory, found clean clothes, dressed, and raced downstairs. She arrived in the front hall as everyone was coming out of the dining room. Mrs. Neave, carrying some books, was shepherding a group of older girls toward the front classroom. Mary Ann burst into their midst and confronted the teacher.

"Mrs. Neave! It wasn't Jenny's fault! Let her come back – please!"

Mrs. Neave paused, and Mary Ann quailed at her expression.

The girls watched with obvious interest. Mrs. Neave waved them toward the classroom. "Go and sit down and begin reading Chapter Two."

She drew Mary Ann away from the busy hall, into her office.

"*Never* run and shout like that in public, Mary Ann," she said.

"But, Mrs. Neave, why did you dismiss Jenny?" Mary Ann felt overwhelmed with guilt.

"I should have thought that was obvious. She is untrustworthy, dishonest, and quite unfit to work in an establishment such as this."

"But it was *me*! *My* fault!" Mary Ann twisted her hands together and struggled not to cry.

"Jenny is an adult, Mary Ann. You were certainly at fault, but you must not blame yourself for what has happened to her."

"But she won't be able to get another job!" She

knew Jenny must have left without a reference.

"That is not my concern," said Mrs. Neave. And she added, "I've had my eye on Jenny Bolt for some time."

Mary Ann wondered what she meant; whether it was something to do with the pillowcases. Perhaps Jenny *had* taken them.

"Her sister is ill – dying," she said. "And her mother drinks, and Jenny buys medicine for Dinah and looks after them all. I know. I went to their house. If she…if she *took* anything it would have been for her sister."

Mrs. Neave sighed. "I know she was your friend, Mary Ann, and your concern does you credit, but believe me, I was obliged to dismiss her. Go off to your class now. Arithmetic, isn't it? I'm afraid you have missed breakfast. If you feel hungry perhaps it will remind you to be more careful of your behavior in the future. And I must consider what your punishment is to be. We'll speak later this morning."

In the garden, during the break after lunch, Sophia, Lucy and Phoebe clustered around and clamored to know everything. They were astonished at Mary Ann's adventures and hugely impressed by her account of how much she had earned.

"You *sang* at Ranelagh and earned all that!" exclaimed Sophia. "And you never told us what you were going to do! You *toad*!" she added, affectionately.

"I wish we'd known!" said Lucy.

"You'd have been in trouble, then, like me." Mary Ann bit her lip. "And Jenny."

"Oh! About Jenny…" Phoebe looked important: the bearer of news. They all turned to her. "Charlotte Cross told me she overheard Mrs. Price and Cook talking about Jenny. They said she'd been stealing: things had been disappearing from the linen room for months."

"*Months?*"

So that was what Mrs. Neave had been hinting at. Was it true? And what things? They couldn't all have been for Dinah, surely? Mary Ann's trust in Jenny began to waver. And yet Jenny had been kind to her, and honest; she couldn't believe she was no more than a common thief. And even if she was, did that make it right for Mary Ann to betray her?

Her confusion over Jenny was bewildering. But at least the other girls were full of sympathy for *her*. On Mrs. Neave's orders Mary Ann was confined to the house for the rest of term, obliged to read and copy out improving texts, and banned from the garden and from taking part in Saturday outings. Only church on Sundays was permitted. She was quite a heroine, however – escaping from robbers, admired by the grand people at Ranelagh. And the school still had her earnings. Perhaps, Mary Ann thought, when her punishment was over, Mrs. Neave would allow her to stay another half a term for three and a half guineas?

Lucy brought her back to earth. "Will Mrs. Neave tell your parents?"

"I don't know." She had thought of this, but hadn't

dared ask. Her parents would be so angry if they found out. They would probably beat her.

Lucy pondered her own question. "I don't think she will. I don't think she would want them to know that you had been so badly supervised."

That was a cheering thought – and probably true, Mary Ann thought.

But next morning, during French Conversation, Mrs. Price called for Mary Ann and said that she was wanted in the office.

"You have visitors," she said.

CHAPTER FOURTEEN

Mary Ann on Trial

Mary Ann knocked timidly on Mrs. Neave's door.

Visitors, Mrs. Price had said. It could only be her parents, summoned by Mrs. Neave, come to chastise and humiliate her. Even worse, they would be angry with Mrs. Neave, as Lucy had said. Suppose there was an argument? Her father would be sure to shout. I shan't be able to bear it, she thought, if my father makes a fuss and people hear.

"Come in," said Mrs. Neave.

Two women sat in the visitors' chairs. One was Mary Ann's mother. For a moment Mary Ann did not recognize the sharp-faced older woman wearing an elegant but slightly old-fashioned hat. Then she exclaimed, "Grandmama!" and dropped a curtsy. Her mind was racing. Why was her grandmother here? Was the whole family to be involved in her disgrace? It would be too dreadful to bear.

She was surprised when her grandmother looked her up and down with evident approval.

"You've grown," she said.

People always said that. But Mary Ann realized that her grandmother had not seen her for…how long was it? Two years? Three? Mrs. Causey looked much the same, but Mary Ann realized that she herself must have changed greatly.

Mrs. Causey stood up. "Let me look at you. Walk over there." She turned to Mrs. Neave. "Well, she is quite the young lady! Is this your work, Mrs. Neave?"

"We encourage good comportment and manners," said Mrs. Neave, smiling benignly at Mary Ann.

"Mary Ann is very happy here," added her mother, also with a fond glance.

Mary Ann was bewildered. This was not at all what she had expected. Why was everyone so amiable? Had Mrs. Neave not told them, after all? Was she about to do so?

Mary Ann composed her face into a mask of demure submission – suitable, she hoped, for whatever might come next.

"The child's happiness is not essential," said Mrs. Causey, in response to her daughter – and Mary Ann tensed – "but nevertheless I am glad to hear it. Do you work hard, Mary Ann?"

This remark, addressed suddenly to her, startled Mary Ann. "Yes!" she said breathlessly. "Yes, of course, Grandmama."

"No 'of course' about it," retorted her grandmother. "Your mother was as idle as a cat at your age."

"Mama!" protested Mary Ann's mother.

Mary Ann gazed at the floorboards and Mrs. Neave intervened smoothly, "We are all very pleased with Mary Ann. She works hard at her lessons, and is particularly gifted at music."

"Ah, yes, the music!" said Mrs. Causey. "I must hear you sing, Mary Ann."

Mary Ann experienced a moment of panic: here? Now? But it seemed not, for Mrs. Neave said, "Mrs. Causey, I suggest that I take you and Mrs. Giffard on a tour of the school, and show you Mary Ann's work books. And I'm sure Mrs. Corelli would be delighted to play the harpsichord to accompany her singing. Would you like to take tea first?"

They agreed. Mrs. Neave rang for the maid and ordered tea, then asked them to excuse her while she went to speak to the teachers. Mary Ann was left alone with her mother and grandmother. She looked cautiously from one to another of them. Did they know? If they didn't, she was not going to tell them.

"You must be surprised to see us here together," her mother began. Her voice sounded strained. "As you know, I have never liked to ask for help—"

"But common sense has at last prevailed," interrupted Mrs. Causey. "Your mother wrote and told me of your father's financial incompetence and asked me for help with your school fees."

As they spoke Mary Ann felt her anxiety dropping away and her spirits lifting. This was nothing to do with the Ranelagh episode. Her grandmother was going to pay for her to stay on at school!

"Of course, before I could agree to do so," her grandmother continued, "I wanted to see your school and your work, which is why we are here. I need to know that my investment in you will be worthwhile."

At this moment the tea arrived, followed by Mrs. Neave carrying a pile of school books and some drawings that Mary Ann had done in her art class.

Mary Ann shrank with embarrassment and a fear that her work would not be considered good enough.

But Mrs. Neave, all charm and confidence, evidently had no such worries as she showed her pupil's work.

While her grandmother looked through the books and murmured approval, Mary Ann glanced gratefully at her mother. She knew what it must have cost her to ask for help from Grandmama. Although her mother never spoke against their grandmother, Harriet had told Mary Ann that Grandmama disapproved not only of their father but of almost every other choice their mother had made.

Mrs. Giffard sat quietly now, letting Mrs. Causey do the talking, and scarcely taking part in the discussion about Mary Ann's work. She was not at all her usual self; she always dwindled in her mother's presence. Mary Ann remembered, with a pang of guilt, how she had thought that her mother didn't care about her, only about Harriet. It wasn't true. She almost reached out and took her mother's hand – but that would have been too embarrassing in public. Instead she gave a small smile, and her mother responded in the same way.

When Mrs. Causey had declared herself satisfied with Mary Ann's schoolwork and drawing ("adequate" was how she described her granddaughter's sketching ability) they all went upstairs to the music room, where Mrs. Corelli was waiting for them. Nervously, Mary Ann played one of the harpsichord pieces Mr. Ashton had taught her; and then Mrs. Corelli put "When Daisies Pied and Violets Blue" on the music stand, and Mary Ann sang to her accompaniment. Her voice, when she began, was tremulous. Not only was she anxious to impress but she had done a lot of crying in the last day or so and felt quite hoarse. But Mrs. Corelli caught her eye and smiled encouragingly, and soon she was singing with confidence.

As she finished with the chorus of "cuckoos" – one after another sung by her and echoed by the harpsichord – she saw her grandmother smile. Mrs. Neave smiled too and said, "Mary Ann will sing that song, and others, I believe, at our concert in September. She is one of our most gifted singers. We are delighted to have her in the choir."

Mrs. Causey looked pleased, and Mrs. Neave, encouraged, went on, "We take the girls to a concert at Ranelagh every year, where they can hear the very best musicians and singers and observe genteel behavior. This year we were fortunate enough to see the Mozart children perform."

"Oh, Grandmama, it was such a wonderful occasion!" Mary Ann broke in without thinking. "I do so long to perform like Miss Mozart!"

Mrs. Causey's expression changed. "I hope you do not think of performing in public, Mary Ann?"

"Oh! No – of course not…" Mary Ann lowered her eyes modestly and was silent.

"It is not necessary, or even desirable, for a lady to excel," said her grandmother. "Tell me, Mary Ann, what *do* you consider to be the purpose of your education here?"

Mary Ann knew she had to give the right answer.

Her fate might depend upon it.

"To acquire ladylike accomplishments and learn how to converse and behave in society."

"To what end?"

"To make a good marriage."

"Indeed." Her grandmother scrutinized Mary Ann's face, as if suspecting her of wanting more. Then she turned to her daughter. "Well, Susan, I have no wish to see my granddaughter disadvantaged by her father's folly. I shall be pleased to pay for her education at Mrs. Neave's school for as long as necessary."

"Oh!" Mary Ann thought she had never felt so happy. There were smiles and thanks all around, and even as she stammered out her own genuine gratitude she saw how her grandmother relished this moment of power.

"Let me make clear," Mrs. Causey said sternly, "that there must be no talk of performing on the stage – nowhere more public than the school concert or a friend's drawing room. Your singing is intended to be an ornament, Mary Ann, not a calling. Do you understand?"

"Yes, Grandmama," said Mary Ann.

All her friends were delighted with Mary Ann's news. That evening, as they sat and chatted in the dormitory, Mary Ann pulled out the charity concert ticket from its hiding place in the paneling, and gazed at the picture. She still loved Ranelagh, in spite of her last experience. She thought of those singers in their silk gowns and powdered hair, and of Maria Anna Mozart. One day, she thought, I'll sing there, in the Rotunda. I'll be on that stage, under those glittering chandeliers, and the applause will be for me.

"Lights out, girls!" called Mrs. Corelli.

Mary Ann pushed the ticket back into its place – but this time it slipped right inside, out of reach! She picked at the edge of it with her fingernail, but only succeeded in pushing it further in. She hunted for a hairpin.

"What's the matter?" asked Sophia.

"My Ranelagh ticket. It's gone into the paneling."

Sophia produced tweezers, but it was no good. She had lost it. The ticket was visible, but quite out of reach.

Like my ambition to sing at the opera, thought Mary Ann. Perhaps one day…but for now she knew she must keep her dreams secret.

CHAPTER FIFTEEN

Many Voices

Dear Sis, wrote George, *What excellent news! Imagine the old girl coming up with the money like that! I wonder how long she and Mama will stay friends? She is quite a dragon, I recall (better burn this after reading). Papa must be furious. I wish I'd been at home when Mama told him what she'd done! I suppose by the time he found out, it was too late to prevent it. He never mentioned it to me in his last letter, but it seems he has become involved in another likely venture, so his mind will be on that. Perhaps this time he will make our fortunes, and then Hatty can find another suitor and spurn the odious Mr. Browne.*

What is this escapade of yours that you hint at? Is it really so dreadful that you can only whisper the details to me when next we meet? Surely not?

Alas, dear Sis, much as I'd love to hear you sing, I shall be in the midst of examinations on that date. Greek and Latin call. Be good – and remember me to Grandmama.

Your loving brother,

George

Dear George, wrote Mary Ann. Really you should not be so rude about Grandmama. I believe that at heart she is kind, and probably also rather lonely. As she lives nearby, in Kensington, she has promised to call occasionally on a Saturday and take me out. I shall introduce her to the Bun House; and she says she may take me to see the royal tombs in Westminster Abbey.

Harriet writes with good news. Her friend Elizabeth

Dunn is traveling with an aunt to Paris, where they will stay for six weeks, and Harriet is invited to go with them! She is hugely excited and glad to be away from all the gossip about her and Mr. Browne. She says she would not have Mr. Browne now if he were to beg her on bended knee.

I should be jealous of Harriet's good fortune were I not so happy here. We are busy practicing for our concert, and we also go outside often in the fine weather. And, George, you will never guess! The Mozart family is staying here, in Chelsea — quite near us, in Five Fields Row — and Sophia and I saw them in the street while we were out walking: Mrs. Mozart, that is, and Wolfgang and Nannerl! We were so very delighted! I am much taken with Nannerl's looks. She is of a height similar to mine, and fair, like me, but much prettier. I am trying to do my hair in the same style as hers; Sophia helps me. Mrs. Corelli heard that Mr. Mozart has been ill and so they have taken lodgings here because the air is fresher than in London; but they have given no concerts for several weeks and none is planned till he recovers. Mrs. Corelli says it is a *chancy profession. I think she intended that remark as a warning to me.*

Mary Ann paused, and put down her pen. She had also seen someone else she knew that day, while walking back to the school. It had been market day, and the voices of the fruit, vegetable and flower sellers competed with each other in a tangle of sing-song calls:

"Buy my sweet lavender!"

"Plums! Juicy plums! Fresh picked today!"

"A rose, sir? A red rose for your sweetheart?"

And then Mary Ann had heard another voice – one she knew well: "Apples! Ripe red apples! First of the season!"

It was Jenny. She stood behind a stand piled high with fruit, singing out her wares in that clear, musical voice that Mary Ann remembered. She was a queen of the market: tall, dark-eyed, fine-looking even in her simple dress and coarse apron. There was an older woman on the same stand; not her mother – her employer, Mary Ann supposed. Jenny was clearly good for trade with her voice and good looks. She saw Mary Ann, caught her eye, and smiled, widening her eyes in surprise.

Mary Ann approached the stand.

"You're still at school, then, Miss?" Jenny said.

"Oh, yes! My grandmother –"

But it was impossible to talk. Jenny turned away to serve a customer, filling a bag with apples.

"I'm sorry," Mary Ann said, when Jenny turned back to her. "I tried to tell Mrs. Neave…"

Jenny shrugged. "I prefer the market – not so many rules! And I wait tables at the Duke of York and sing there some evenings. All I want now is better lodgings. Yes, sir? Can I help you?"

She smiled and moved away, and Mary Ann left and returned to her friends. She felt great relief. Jenny didn't blame her for what had happened. And she had found work, despite not being given a reference by Mrs. Neave. Mary Ann didn't care what others said about Jenny;

Jenny had been a good friend to her, whatever else she'd done. She, Mary Ann, was the one who had let her friend down and caused her to be dismissed…

She continued her letter to George: *The program for our concert will be printed tomorrow. I am to be on first, after the choir have sung "Nymphs and Shepherds." Think of me before you go in to your examination — and I'll think of you.*

With love, your sister,

Mary Ann

"I need the lavatory again," said Sophia.

It was the day of the concert, and the girls were in the dormitory, making sure they had handkerchiefs and fans, that there were no holes in their stockings, no scuff marks on their silk slippers. The outhouses were two flights down, in the back yard. They had all been lining up there earlier, for a long time.

"It's only nerves," said Lucy. "You can't join that line again."

She and Phoebe were more relaxed, as they merely had their work on show and were not performing.

"The audience is starting to arrive," said Phoebe. She led them out to look down through the central drop in the stairwell to a narrow segment of checkered hall floor far below. No visitors were visible, but Mary Ann could hear their voices: a hum of pleased anticipation.

"We'll be called down soon," said Phoebe.

Sophia clutched herself. "I *have* to go again!"

"Use the pot," said Mary Ann. "We'll wait out here."

Sophia darted into the dormitory.

Mary Ann felt the same mixture of nervousness and excitement. I wonder if professional performers feel like this, she thought; or do they get used to it?

Earlier that day they had seen the two downstairs front rooms transformed for the occasion. The dining room was full of tables draped in white linen on which were displayed the best examples of the girls' work in writing, French composition, sewing, drawing and painting. Across the hall, the front classroom had been cleared of its globe, wall displays and desks, and set out with chairs for both audience and performers. The harpsichord from the dining room had been brought in and placed near the window. Both rooms were full of flowers, and the smell of roses, mingled with the visitors' perfumes, floated up the stairwell.

The girls all wore pale summer gowns, and Mary Ann and her friends had arranged each other's hair. Mary Ann hoped hers looked like Nannerl Mozart's. Mrs. Corelli had briefly inspected them all earlier and given her approval.

Sophia came back. They looked down the stairwell, but saw only the heads of other girls also looking down. The sounds from below were fainter now. The audience must all be seated. Mary Ann felt light-headed with nerves.

Then came the sound of Mr. Ashton playing the harpsichord. That was their signal. Mrs. Corelli appeared on the stairs, and they followed her down and joined the girls from the second floor. They all filed into the concert room to take their places, either with the choir or along the sides of the room.

Mary Ann, Sophia, and the other soloists sat in the front row of the choir. Sophia gripped Mary Ann's hand. "I shall faint!" she whispered melodramatically.

Mrs. Neave stood up to speak to the audience. Mary Ann heard scarcely anything of what she said; she was too nervous and too busy scanning the audience for her family. Heads, hats, feathers, flickering fans... *There* they were, in the center: Mama, Grandmama, Harriet – and Papa! She was surprised to see her father – especially with Grandmama, whom she knew he disliked. Perhaps Mama had talked him into coming. Dear Mama, she thought, she has been so kind to me; she must have hated going to Grandmama for help. And yet the two of them were chatting and smiling together now, and even Papa appeared to be at his most amiable. She caught her sister's eye and gave a little wave, and Harriet waved back.

And then Mrs. Neave finished talking, and moved to the side, and Mr. Ashton began to play. The choir stood up to the introduction to "Nymphs and Shepherds."

Singing with the choir calmed Mary Ann's nerves; there was safety in the mingled voices:

"Nymphs and shepherds, come away,

Come away…"

When the song was over the audience applauded warmly, with smiles and cheers; and a plump, magnificently red-haired lady who could only be Sophia's mother, called out, "Bravo!"

Then the clapping died away, and Mrs. Corelli nodded to Mary Ann, who stood up and walked out in front. From the harpsichord came the introduction to Galatea's air. Mary Ann sang:

"As when the dove

Laments her love,

All on the naked spray;

When he returns,

No more she mourns,

But love the live-long day…"

She heard the notes in her head, and they came out as she heard them: perfect. She relaxed, and forgot her nerves, and sang for the joy of it.

When she sat down, and the applause began, she thought: I shall always have this. Even if I don't sing at Covent Garden, don't become famous; no matter what happens to me I shall have the music and it will always make me happy.

But she would not give up her dreams – not yet.

She looked out at her family and smiled.

AUTHOR'S NOTE

Mary Ann's story will take you back to 1764 – a time when Chelsea was a village on the outskirts of London. At that date Number Six, Chelsea Walk, was closer to the river because the Embankment (a bank that was built up along the north side of the River Thames to reclaim marshy land) had not yet been built.

Visitors were drawn to Chelsea by the popularity of Ranelagh Gardens. The concert in this story really did take place, and the young Wolfgang Amadeus Mozart was one of the performers. In 1764 Mozart and his sister Nannerl were performing regularly together in London. I can find no proof that Nannerl was also at

Ranelagh that day, but as the two children usually appeared together it seems likely that she was. Their father promoted his children as prodigies and in his advertisements he actually knocked a year off each child's age to make them seem even more amazing. In this story they are given their real ages. Nannerl Mozart was a brilliant musician who was gradually overshadowed by the genius of her younger brother.

The songs Mary Ann sings were all popular at the time, and are still sung. I used to sing some of them in my school choir in the 1950s!

I hope you will enjoy reading this story and meeting another of the girls who have lived at 6 Chelsea Walk.

Ann Turnbull

ABOUT THE AUTHOR

Ann Turnbull knew from an early age that she wanted to be a writer. After working as a secretary for many years, Ann returned to studying and started to train as a teacher. It was then that she rediscovered children's literature and began writing for children herself. Her first novel was published in 1974 and she is now a full-time author. She has written more than thirty books for children and young adults, including *Pigeon Summer* and *No Shame, No Fear*, which have both been shortlisted for prestigious UK children's book awards.

Ann lives with her husband in Shropshire, England.

To find out more about Ann Turnbull, you can visit her website: www.annturnbull.com.

USBORNE QUICKLINKS

For links to websites where you can listen to music from Mary Ann's time and find out more about the Mozart children and Ranelagh Gardens, go to the Usborne Quicklinks website at www.usborne.com/quicklinks and type in the title of this book.

At Usborne Quicklinks you can:

- Listen to songs Mary Ann loved to sing
- Watch a musician play a harpsichord and find out how it works
- See some of the fashions of the day
- Find out more about everyday life in the 1700s

Please follow the online safety guidelines at the Usborne Quicklinks website.

6 Chelsea Walk

1857

Girls

with

Courage

ADÈLE GERAS

USBORNE

To Debra Armstrong

Contents

6 CHELSEA WALK, 1857

Basement

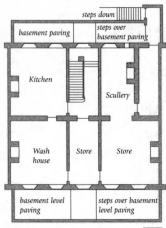

steps down
basement paving
steps over basement paving
Kitchen
Scullery
Wash house
Store
Store
basement level paving
steps over basement level paving

First-floor

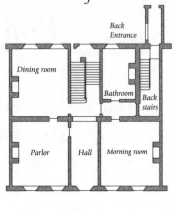

Back Entrance
Dining room
Bathroom
Back stairs
Parlor
Hall
Morning room

Second-floor

Library
Bathroom
Back stairs
Drawing room
Clara's bedroom
Grandmama's bedroom

Third-floor

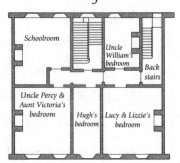

Schoolroom
Uncle William's bedroom
Back stairs
Uncle Percy & Aunt Victoria's bedroom
Hugh's bedroom
Lucy & Lizzie's bedroom

Roof space

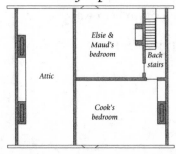

Elsie & Maud's bedroom
Back stairs
Attic
Cook's bedroom

CHAPTER ONE

Lizzie Frazer prepares for a journey

Lizzie was packing her suitcase, ready for her visit to London. Even though she knew how much she would miss Mama, she was looking forward to the journey; to seeing her cousins again and to living for a time in the fine house in Chelsea about which she had heard so much, and which she was sure was a great deal larger than their cottage. Uncle Percy was the owner of a prosperous fabric shop, and the house, so Mama said, was decorated in the most up-to-date style. Uncle Percy was the richest of the three Frazer brothers, and Lizzie didn't mind that, but it had always struck her as somehow unjust that her beloved father should have been the one brother to die young. Uncle Percy was the eldest, and Uncle William was a soldier who had fought in the recent war in the Crimea, and both of them, in Lizzie's opinion, should therefore have been much more likely to leave this earth before their time than her papa, John Frazer.

He had died when Lizzie was only five, from a fever resulting from a bad chill, but even though seven years had passed since then, she remembered her father well, or thought she did. She could summon up memories of walking with him through the woods near their small house, where he would point at the plants and flowers, and tell her their names. If she shut her eyes, she could see a picture in her mind of herself, scarcely more than a baby, sitting on his broad shoulders and looking down at the world, with her head (that was what it felt like) almost touching the clouds.

More and more often lately, Lizzie needed to remind herself of those happy days. Her mother was now married to Mr. Eli Bright, a curate at the village church. He had moved into their cottage, not having a great deal of wealth of his own. Mama explained to Lizzie that now she was married to Mr. Bright, her money and possessions quite naturally became his. This seemed most unfair to Lizzie, and in her opinion Mama's new husband had turned their home into a chilly sort of place, where laughter was frowned on and every kind of comfort denied. Her mother scarcely ever played the piano as she used to, and the lamps seemed to glow with a far dimmer light than they had in the days when Papa was alive. How it was that her mother, Cecily Frazer, who was so lively, pretty and gentle, could find it in her heart to love someone as gloomy, strict and unfeeling as Eli Bright was beyond Lizzie's understanding, and she dared not ask, for fear of reminding Mama of everything she was missing. She resolved not to think about such matters for the moment, but instead to look forward to her journey to London.

Lizzie had decided to take all three of her dresses with her. One was made of blue wool and had lace trimmings at the cuffs and collar. Another was brown serge; Lizzie thought it sadly plain and only suitable for school. Her Sunday dress was moss-green velvet and rather old. She hoped she would not grow too tall for it before it was quite worn out. She was also taking two white pinafores: the ones that had been mended less often than the others. She had chosen a book or two to accompany her on her travels and her *Mother Goose Rhymes* had a few precious flowers from the garden pressed between the pages.

All her belongings were neatly laid out on the bed in her tiny bedroom, and Mama was helping her to fold everything and put it into the suitcase. Lizzie was enjoying this rare opportunity for private conversation with her mother. Mr. Bright (Lizzie refused to call him Father, and Eli, his Christian name, was too familiar) was always present and ready to overhear whatever they said to one another when they were downstairs. She knew that it was his idea that she should be sent away from home. Her mother was expecting a baby soon after Christmas, and Mr. Bright considered that Lizzie's departure would make life much easier for his wife.

"I wish I might be allowed to stay here in the country with you, Mama," Lizzie said. "I wish I didn't have to leave you alone with Mr. Bright. He doesn't seem very happy about the baby." She didn't say so to Mama, but she had noticed that since her mother had announced her pregnancy, Mr. Bright had taken to reading his Bible in private for hours at a time, and made even less effort to converse with them at mealtimes than he ever had.

"No, dear, you may be sure he is delighted. Eli is very anxious that I should be spared too much hard work. That is all."

Lizzie wanted to protest that her own presence in the cottage ought not to be called "hard work." Indeed, she was the one (since Annie, the maid, was rather slow and elderly) who helped her mother with the cooking and the laundry and the dusting of the few ornaments that Mr. Bright permitted them to display. It occurred to her also that if Eli Bright was delighted by anything, he had managed to hide it from everyone.

"Your Uncle Percy is kindness itself," Mama continued. "He has always been a good brother-in-law to me, and it's kind of him to offer you a home until after the baby is born. His new house is very grand, I believe, but quite full already. All three children still live at home, as well as your Grandmama Henrietta and Uncle William. To say nothing of Uncle Percy and Aunt Victoria themselves, of course. And the servants. You will be a crowd, there is no doubt of it. He's found room for you, Lizzie, and you must be aware of that kindness and be polite and helpful at all times…"

"I will, Mama. I promise. And I'll write to you,

so that you may know about the fine sights which will be all around me in Chelsea."

Lizzie could see that her mother was blinking tears away from her eyes, and indeed, she herself was beginning to feel sad at the thought of leaving, so she changed the subject as quickly as she could.

"I must find room for this, Mama," she said, holding out a tin box which had once contained tea. She had tied string around it, as carefully as she could, so that it would not fly open while she was traveling.

"What have you got in there, child?" Mama asked. "I'm sure Uncle Percy has tea in plenty and you've no need to take such things with you."

"It's not tea," said Lizzie. "It's something else. It's private."

"Will you not tell me your secret? Otherwise, I might do nothing but wonder and wonder, after you've left us."

"It's a walnut in a flowerpot. I took one of the finest-looking nuts, still in its husk, from Mr. Alton's tree when he was harvesting his walnuts and I've planted it in a small flowerpot. I've put the flowerpot into the tea-caddy and it must remain upright during the journey or the earth will fall out. I'll look after it in London, never fear."

"Oh, Lizzie, your papa used to do that…do you remember? Plant a walnut to make a new tree. How can you recall it when you were such a young child?"

Before Lizzie answered, she had to collect herself a little. All of a sudden she was overcome with sadness to think how much she would miss helping Mr. Alton with his trees. He had a large orchard that neighbored their own garden and he was always kind to Lizzie and told her all about the plants and flowers she loved so well.

"It came into my mind when I saw the husks lying on the ground. I wanted to take something with me from home. Something to remind me of the countryside. Mr. Alton gave me the flowerpot. He says I'm to keep it in a cold frame so that it may live through one hard frost before it's ready to sprout. Do you think Uncle Percy has such a thing as a cold frame in his garden?"

"I'm sure I don't know," said Mama. "You'll discover when you get to Chelsea Walk, no doubt. I'll find you a small basket to put your walnut in, so that it may stay upright at all times."

"Thank you, Mama," said Lizzie, and she returned to the folding of her pinafores. She was determined to enjoy all that London had to offer and make Mama proud of her, but it was hard not to feel sad at the thought of leaving home.

CHAPTER TWO

Lizzie meets
her cousins again

Mama, Lizzie could see, was wiping away her tears with a lace-edged handkerchief as the coach left the Huntsman's Inn on its way to London. It was a very grand coach, Lizzie felt, with a handsomely dressed coachman sitting on the high seat and four fine chestnut horses to draw it through the countryside. Lizzie bit her lip hard because she was quite determined to be brave and grown up, no matter how sad and lost she felt on the journey. Saying goodbye to Mama was very hard, and Lizzie tried to concentrate on keeping her basket safely upright, to stop her from thinking of how much she would miss her mother.

Still, it was true that part of her longed to see London and reacquaint herself with her cousins, whom she had not seen for some years. She would miss her friends in the village school, but had no doubt that London schools were full of pleasant girls. Also, she comforted herself with the knowledge that she was not banished from her home forever, but only for a few months. The Frazer family house was near the river, and there would be ships and tall buildings and perhaps they would even pass by Buckingham Palace, which was where Queen Victoria lived with Prince Albert when they were in London.

Lizzie's cousins were named Clara, Lucy and Hugh. Clara was sixteen years old and already a young lady, Mama said. Lucy was only eight, but Hugh was twelve years old, as Lizzie was. He would doubtless be her closest companion. Lizzie sighed. That couldn't be helped of course, but boys, from what she had seen, had too good an opinion of themselves and never allowed that a girl might have a mind of her own.

Uncle William had returned from the Crimean battlefields, Mama told her, "utterly changed." She knew this from letters Uncle Percy had written to her, for Mama, too, had not visited London for many years. As Lizzie had never met Uncle William, perhaps she wouldn't notice the difference, but whenever Mama spoke of him, she sighed and shook her head and said how terrible the war had been, and how we must give devout thanks that William had come back from it with his limbs intact, even if he had lost one eye. Lizzie had been shown where the Crimea was on the globe, and told that our soldiers were helping the Serbs to fight against the Russians, but it had all appeared to be taking place a long way away, on the other side of the world, and Lizzie had had no clear idea why everyone should be at war with everyone else. Perhaps Uncle William would be able to explain it all to her.

Lizzie gazed out of the window as the coach traveled through the countryside for nearly an hour. Gradually, the trees and hedges gave way to paved streets. After another half hour or so, the coach approached central London. Lizzie's six fellow passengers craned their necks to look out of the window, and she did the same. Soon, they were in the heart of the city. There were fine, tall buildings everywhere and the wide, paved streets were full of people and carriages. The coach drove swiftly past houses and shops and Lizzie thought that no matter how long she stayed here she would never grow used to the noise and the bustle of the hurrying crowds.

Uncle Percy was there to meet her at the coaching inn. She remembered him from the last time she'd visited London, even though that had been six years ago, when she and Mama came to see the Great Exhibition at the Crystal Palace. He hadn't changed, and was still just as portly and red-faced as ever, but Lizzie was sure her cousins would be greatly altered. Uncle Percy shouted out as she stepped down from the coach, "Lizzie, my dear! It is you, isn't it? To be sure it is. How very grown up you are! Follow me, follow me. Our carriage is waiting and we shall soon be home. The children are eager to make your acquaintance once again."

"Thank you, Uncle Percy," said Lizzie, remembering what her mother had told her and curtseying a little to add to the politeness that she hoped was in her voice. Uncle Percy seized her suitcase in his big hand and Lizzie tucked her basket carefully over her arm, ever careful of the flowerpot she was carrying within it, and followed him to where the carriage was waiting. Lizzie began to feel a little apprehensive at the thought of what awaited her in Chelsea. She felt tired and grubby from the journey and hoped that her cousins wouldn't think her a country bumpkin. She resolved to smile when she was introduced to her cousins and be as friendly as she could to make up for her disheveled appearance.

The house in Chelsea Walk was even grander than Lizzie had imagined. It was very near the river. As soon as Uncle Percy pointed the water out to her, she longed to go and stand on the Embankment and watch the ships passing on their way down to the sea, or to the docks.

"Very well-connected people live in Chelsea," he told Lizzie. "The late Mr. Turner, the artist, you know, was almost a neighbor of ours for a while. And do you see that church? That is the Old Church, where we worship on Sundays."

The Frazers' house was built of red brick. With the basement, there were five stories altogether, and it seemed very tall indeed to Lizzie. There was a wrought-iron gate which stood about waist-high to Uncle Percy and railings also in wrought iron to separate the front garden from the street. Three wide steps led up to the door. Lizzie wished Mama could have seen such splendor. I miss her already, she thought. How I wish that Mr. Bright might vanish altogether so that I could go home!

She blinked hard to prevent tears from falling, and told herself not to be such a ninny. London was the capital of the country, the hub of the Empire and full of interesting sights and people. It was ungrateful of her to wish herself elsewhere, when Uncle Percy and Aunt Victoria were being so kind.

The whole family was waiting in the front parlor to greet her. Lizzie gazed around the room in astonishment. She felt sure that the whole of Mama's cottage could have fit into it, with some space left over. How fine the furnishings were! The paneling was dark wood and there were curtains of olive-green plush at the window. Several carpets were spread over the polished wooden floors and these had patterns of trees and flowers and fruit woven into them. It seemed to Lizzie a shame that they had to be trodden by people's feet. If they were mine, she thought, I'd hang them on the wall and gaze at their colors all day long.

"This is your cousin Elizabeth, children," said Uncle Percy. "Clara, you will remember her last visit, and you, too, Hugh, but Lucy, you were only two years old. All you children have changed a great deal in the last six years." He turned to Lizzie and smiled. "I'm sure that you recall your Aunt Victoria and your grandmother, however. They have scarcely changed at all."

Lizzie felt her cheek kissed by her aunt. She was thin, with a kind smile and soft hands, and she was wearing a dress in dark blue wool with a lace collar at the neck. Her grandmother, Mrs. Henrietta Frazer, was a short, stout person, who rather resembled the Queen, and dressed to emphasize the likeness, in a gray bombazine dress trimmed with braid.

"Welcome to London, child," said Mrs. Frazer. "You may call me Grandmama like the others, I suppose."

"Thank you, Grandmama," said Lizzie.

"How is dear Cecily's health?" Grandmama asked.

"Thank you, she is as well as can be expected," Lizzie answered and wondered what on earth she could think of to say next. Fortunately, Uncle Percy was busy bringing the others forward and Lizzie found herself face to face with a tall, young woman. This must be Cousin Clara, Lizzie thought. She was very pretty, with glossy, dark brown hair and kind, smiling eyes.

"How do you do?" she said. "I'm your Cousin Clara. I don't suppose you have any recollection of the occasion because it was so long ago, but I was the one looking after you when you visited the Great Exhibition. Do you remember?"

"Oh, yes," said Lizzie. "I thought that the whole exhibition was nothing but a forest of skirts and trousers because that was all I could see, till you lifted me up."

"Yes, I remember," Clara said with a laugh. "You were very heavy for me and I handed you to Papa after a little while." Her smile made Lizzie feel properly at home for the first time.

"This is Lucy," said Uncle Percy, moving her on to where her youngest cousin was sitting in a small armchair. Lucy's pinafore was very white indeed and her shoes were polished to a high shine. She wore a dark red ribbon in her hair, which curled in ringlets onto her shoulders. Lizzie thought that she might have been called pretty if she'd had a more agreeable expression on her face.

"You're very small indeed for someone who is twelve years old," said Lucy. Lizzie would have liked to answer: *And you are quite old enough to have some manners*, but she recalled what she'd promised her mother and looked down at her feet instead.

"Stop being so rude," Lucy's brother told his little sister, stepping forward and shaking Lizzie by the hand. His sandy-colored hair fell almost into his eyes and he pushed it back with one hand. "I'm Hugh. Take no notice of Lucy. She may be the youngest, but she's always giving herself airs."

"Children, children," said Aunt Victoria mildly. "There must be no quarrels or disagreeable talk on Lizzie's first day here. What will she think of us? Hugh, you may show Lizzie around the house presently, but Elsie will be here in a moment with the tea."

Just then, the door to the parlor flew open and a tall, dark man with a scowl on his face and a black patch over one eye came into the room. He glanced neither to right nor left, but strode to the window and remained gazing out at the street. He seemed to disturb the air as he went, and leave a kind of shadow behind him. Hugh, who was standing close to Lizzie, bent to whisper in her ear.

"Poor old Uncle William does get angry very easily. It's as well to keep out of his way when he's in a temper."

"What makes him angry?" Lizzie whispered back.

"It's hard to know exactly," said Hugh. "Anything might. Best to avoid him altogether."

"William, dear," said Aunt Victoria. "This is Cecily's girl, Elizabeth. Lizzie. She's come to stay with us for a while. Won't that be delightful?"

Lizzie trembled at the idea that Uncle William might come over to greet her and shake her hand. How would she bear to look at that dreadful patch? Even the glimpse she'd had of it as Uncle William crossed the room had caused her to shudder. She imagined what was underneath it (a great hole of blackness where his eye had been) and knew that it would give her nightmares for a long time to come. But Uncle William didn't move or turn around. Lizzie thought she heard a grunt coming from his direction, but it was difficult to be sure. Aunt Victoria seemed much relieved when Elsie, the maid, came in carrying the tea tray. Lizzie looked at her uncle's back and shivered. He seemed so angry and unhappy that she felt a sadness come over her as she thought about him. He did not take his tea with the rest of the family but remained at his post by the window, gazing at the twilight until Elsie came in to draw the curtains and take away the tea things.

Lizzie felt suddenly very tired and wondered how long it would be before she was able to go upstairs and unpack. She tried not to think about what Mama might be doing, because she was quite determined not to cry after everyone had been so kind to her.

CHAPTER THREE

Lizzie writes
a letter home

October 25th, 1857.

Dearest Mama,
This is a very fine house, Lizzie wrote, *and it will
take me some time to grow used to it, when I have
known only our little home till yesterday. There is
a parlor and a drawing room and a dining room and
a library and bedrooms on the upper floors and in*

the attic, and the kitchen and scullery and washhouse down in the basement and all the public rooms and the bedrooms very finely decorated in the most modern style...

Lizzie was sitting at the table in the schoolroom with Lucy on her first morning in London. It had once been a nursery, but the Frazer children had grown too old to be looked after by a nanny. Clara had left school and was now learning to be a lady in the company of her mother and grandmother. Hugh went to a boys' school at Westminster and Lucy attended Miss Jenkins's Academy, near Sloane Square. Aunt Victoria had arranged for Lizzie to have lessons there as well, while she was in London. Hugh studied Latin and Science and Geography, and Lizzie wished she might accompany him and not Lucy. At Miss Jenkins's, she was sure, all she would learn was French and Recitation and Bible Studies and how to paint in watercolors. Perhaps if she and Hugh became good friends, she thought, he might teach her some of the things he was learning.

Lizzie had always been allowed to look at her father's books at home. Her particular favorites were the leather-bound volumes full of detailed botanical drawings of every flower and plant imaginable, and she also loved *Gulliver's Travels* and *The Pilgrim's Progress*. She remembered the terrible day when Mr. Bright had decided that such studies were not becoming to a young lady and forbidden her to take out the books and look at them. When she had disobeyed him, he had sold them to a bookseller and told Lizzie that she would be much better occupied with housework. Of all the dreadful things Mr. Bright had done, this was easily the worst. It wasn't just the books, it was the memories of her father, which Lizzie felt had been torn away from her. Her mother had tried to console her, and promised her that when she was older, she would be allowed to read such things again, but Lizzie remained furious and upset for days.

Hugh had shown her around the house on the previous afternoon, and she was still dizzy from thinking about the number of rooms and stairs and landings and attics and from trying to remember her way around them all.

I am sharing a bedroom with Lucy, she wrote. *It is on the third floor. Grandmama's bedroom is on the first floor and Elsie and Cook sleep in the attic. So does Maud, the second housemaid. Uncle William's room is across the landing from ours, and Hugh has the small bedroom next to Uncle Percy and Aunt Victoria's. Lucy and Clara used to share, but now I'm here, Clara has moved into her own bedroom.*

Lizzie wondered whether she ought to mention that Lucy had not been very welcoming, but decided against it. She had shown Lizzie the drawers into which she was supposed to put her things, and had made it quite clear that her opinion of the clothes Lizzie took out of her suitcase wasn't very high. She had wrinkled her nose a little and said, "Your dresses are not very pretty. Not as pretty as Clara's. Or mine. I expect that's because you come from the country. Perhaps Papa will find you some clothes that you can wear in London."

Lucy had also noticed the tea-caddy as Lizzie took it from the basket and set it on the chest of drawers.

"What's in there?" she asked, rather rudely.

"It's a walnut in a flowerpot. It will grow into a tree one day."

"Hugh likes things like that," Lucy said, making it clear that she cared not a jot for walnuts or about any plant for that matter. "You ought to tell him about it." She turned her attention to other matters, and didn't mention the contents of the tea-caddy again.

Lizzie's first night in London had been the opposite of peaceful, but she decided not to write that to her mother either. It was sure to worry her. Aunt Victoria had come to wish Lucy and herself good night, and tucked Lizzie in quite kindly. She had even kissed her on the top of her head, but it was not the same at all as Mama's warm embrace. The girls had each brought a candle in a candlestick to light them as they undressed, and Aunt Victoria blew these out before she left. Lizzie feared lying awake, because of being in a strange room and feeling a little homesick, but her tiredness was so great that she fell asleep at once. Then, quite suddenly, she found herself wide awake again and staring into the dark. Lucy was snoring gently, like a cat lying by the fire. Lizzie smiled to herself, and thought how mortified her young cousin would be to know that she'd been overheard doing something as coarse as *snoring*.

That was when Lizzie heard the noise. What was it? A shouting from somewhere, but muffled, as though whoever was making the sounds was covering up his mouth. She sat up at once and gazed around her. She could see the jug and basin on top of the chest of drawers, but it was too dark to make out the rose pattern painted on the china. She could just make out the shape of the armoire against the far wall. A line of light was visible under the door. There it was again: a shout and something that sounded like a sob. Someone was crying.

Lizzie jumped out of bed. She opened the bedroom door as quietly as she could, and understood at once that it was Uncle William who was making those terrible noises. She could hear them quite clearly now. His door was open and someone was with him. There was light coming from his room. Lizzie could hear a voice. Aunt Victoria's? No, it was Grandmama.

"Hush, my baby boy," she said. "You're having a bad dream. See, you are here with us in London and all is well. Nothing to worry yourself over. See now, I've brought you a warm drink. Don't cry, dearest. Take comfort from the fact that you are with your family and we all care for you and love you. There, there…"

Lizzie went back to her bed, and sat listening in the dark. Gradually, the sobs subsided and then faded away altogether. She watched the light from the lamp

Grandmama must have been carrying disappear as she went rather heavily downstairs to her own bedroom.

Then Lizzie lay back against her pillows. Slowly, two tears crept out of her eyes and she wiped them away with a corner of her sheet. She couldn't tell whether she was crying for her own mother, because she missed her, or for poor Uncle William, who had wept like a small child even though he was once a soldier who had served his country with such courage. I must be just as brave as any soldier, she said to herself. Mama would be worried to think of me lying in a fine London bed and crying, so I will stop this instant. Lizzie made a great effort and managed to stem the tears, but it had taken her very many minutes to fall asleep again.

In the schoolroom, Lizzie turned to her letter again: *I think of you all the time, dear Mama, and long for your letters. Be sure to write every day and tell me everything that is happening in the village. The* garden here is very fine, though I miss the red and gold of the leaves on the trees around our cottage. Here, there are many shrubs, and a lawn and a border that will be full of flowers in the summer, but it's not like our garden in the country. Hugh says the gardens at Kew are the best in the whole world. He goes there sometimes and I hope he'll take me one day.

CHAPTER FOUR

Lizzie struggles to become more ladylike

On Lizzie's second day in London, Lucy pulled her cousin by the hand and took her into the morning room.

"Mama," she said. "Lizzie has not brought any needlework with her."

"Perhaps she has left it in the country," said Aunt Victoria, smiling at Lizzie, but raising her eyebrows as though waiting for an answer. She was reclining on a kind of half-sofa, upholstered in sage-green velvet.

"No, Aunt Victoria," Lizzie said. "I've never done any needlework. Except for a little darning. I know how to do that, but Mama says my darns are more like thick scars than smooth sewing."

She could see from the pinching of her mouth that Aunt Victoria was shocked and felt that Lizzie's mother had neglected her education in this matter.

"Not even a sampler?" she asked.

Lizzie shook her head. "No, Aunt Victoria. Not even that."

Her aunt sighed loudly and said, "Well, then, I must help you to begin one, and see that you learn the stitches. I would have expected you, at your age, to have mastered the first steps of the embroidery skills that should be part of every young lady's education. Lucy is only eight years old but finished her first sampler last year. Come and sit beside me and we'll begin on this piece of canvas. Here is your needle, and I will ask Elsie to find a sewing basket for you. I am sure there must be one somewhere that you can use."

Lucy smirked and simpered when her mother's attention was on Lizzie. Aunt Victoria didn't notice, but Lizzie saw her and wished she could put out her tongue at her young cousin.

By the time she and Lucy returned to the schoolroom, Lizzie had decided that embroidery was quite the most tedious occupation in the whole world. She'd sat for an hour or more, dragging a thread of green in a silver needle through the canvas again and again, and all the while she was aware that her cousin and her aunt were sewing away at great speed, making tiny, dainty stitches in the fine linen they were hemming. Aunt Victoria looked over at Lizzie's work and said, "Well, it is your first time, after all. Perhaps it is a mistake to expect too much today. I daresay you will improve with practice."

Lucy was less kind than her mama. Once they were in the schoolroom, she remarked, "Your stitches are too big. My stitches are very small and dainty. Mama said so. She said I am an excellent embroiderer."

"I don't want to be any kind of embroiderer. I hate it. I'd much rather be in the garden with real flowers than making one from threads on a canvas."

"That's because you come from the country, where flowers are more common, I suppose. Here in London, we like our flowers on samplers, in paintings or in vases on the sideboard."

Lizzie wanted to say: *That's very foolish of you. Flowers are best in their natural setting*, but it was almost time for lunch and she didn't want to argue in front of the others, so she remained silent and contented herself with making a face at Lucy's back as she left the room. Lizzie already missed helping Mr. Alton in his orchard and she made up her mind that when she was quite grown up and could do what she pleased, she would find some way to work every day with growing things. She wondered if there were such people in the world as lady gardeners. All the ones she had ever heard of were men.

In the dining room, the whole family sat around an enormous table, covered in a cloth of dazzling white linen. Lizzie was relieved to be seated far away from Uncle William, who stared down at his plate without meeting anyone's gaze. From time to time he took a mouthful of food, but he was deep in his own thoughts. Lizzie wondered why no one tried to speak to him. Perhaps they were as nervous of what he might say as she was. He looked just like a giant in a storybook, hunched over his plate and frowning at the food as though he were displeased by it. She couldn't help fearing that if he were to open his mouth, what would come out would be not words, but terrifying groans and shouts.

Elsie brought in the mutton and vegetables and as soon as she had served everyone, Clara spoke. "I was visiting Papa's shop this morning when Mrs. Barrett came in. She was telling us about Florence Nightingale. She saw her last week, stepping into her carriage. Can you imagine? I should love to make her acquaintance. In fact, I should like to be a nurse myself, and look after the sick and wounded as she did. Mrs. Barrett says that Miss Nightingale has started a school for nurses. I would like more than anything in the world to enroll in that school, Papa. Please, please say that I may approach the hospital – St. Thomas's I believe – and make inquiries. Please?"

Uncle Percy was so taken aback by this remark that he blinked and paused with a forkful of potato halfway to his lips.

"When you were younger, I remember," said Aunt Victoria, putting down her fork and frowning at her daughter, "you did indeed bandage your dolls' limbs, and pretend that your dolls' house was the hospital at Scutari, but your Uncle William was fighting in the Crimea then. It was only natural for you to imagine yourself helping him and others like him. But I think nursing is a most unsuitable profession for a well brought-up young lady."

Clara's cheeks were pink as she answered her mother. "I think the work would suit me."

"Fiddlesticks," said Grandmama, her voice echoing

a little in the high-ceilinged room. "Childish games are a very different matter from the real care of the sick. Just think of the blood, Clara dear. And the possibility of catching so many dreadful diseases. The thought of a grandchild of mine wiping all manner of disgusting *substances* from the faces and bodies of the sick…well, it turns my stomach, I admit it."

Clara whispered under her breath, "But it is not you, Grandmama, who would be attending to the invalids. It would be me, would it not? I know my own mind."

"There is time enough for you to decide such things when you're older," said Uncle Percy. "You are only sixteen years old. We will consider the matter next year, perhaps."

"But surely it would do no harm to make a few inquiries?" Clara asked. Her cheeks were scarlet now and Lizzie could see that she was making a great effort to keep her temper.

"I have no wish to discuss such things at the

moment, Clara," said Aunt Victoria. "We will consider your future again at a later date. For the moment, we must put thoughts of you nursing out of our minds and simply give thanks to Miss Nightingale and her ilk for all their sterling work during the late war."

"She's an angel," said Uncle William, in a voice that sounded to Lizzie as if it were very seldom used. It was harsh and grating as if every word cost Uncle William pain to utter it. "I saw her, you know. At Scutari."

"Indeed you did," said Aunt Victoria, and everyone at the table turned toward Uncle William, eager to see what he said next, but he had fallen silent again, and began to move the food from the plate to his lips once more with a frown on his face.

Clara went on: "I could be an angel like Miss Nightingale. And I wouldn't mind the blood. Nor the vomit. I'm not easily disgusted."

"This is not a fit subject for the lunch table," said Aunt Victoria. "Stop it at once, child. Let us talk about something else."

Lucy was making a horrified face. "Ugh!" she said. "Vomit! Clara, that's disgusting."

"No it's not," said Clara. "It's part of our nature. I'm sure I wouldn't mind that side of it."

"I must return to work," said Uncle Percy. He had finished the food on his plate and put his knife and fork down with a clatter. "I see no reason to continue talking about this matter now, Clara. We will see what the future will bring but for the moment your duty is to learn all the accomplishments that befit a young lady. I'm sure you have a very pleasant life."

"It's pleasant enough, Papa, but not *useful*," said Clara. "I would like to be of some purpose in the world. And I should like to study something more interesting than the latest fashions. Hugh does, and I don't see why I may not."

Lizzie could see that Uncle Percy might have lost his temper, but chose instead to be amused by Clara's outburst. He laughed and said, "Learning indeed! Whatever next? Whoever heard of such a thing?

Besides, Hugh is a boy and a young man must have an education. You will marry in the fullness of time and your duty will be to support and care for your husband. Like your Mama." He smiled at Aunt Victoria.

Hugh, who was sitting opposite Lizzie, said, "I'm going to be a plant collector. I shall study botany and then I'll discover thousands of strange new trees and shrubs and flowers and bring them home to Kew Gardens and they will all be named after me. I won't have time to help Papa in the shop."

Uncle Percy stood up. "Well, this argument will not put bread upon the table. You, Hugh, are very young still and there is time for you to acquire some sense and reason. Your dreams are quite suitable for a child and will change as you grow older, mark my words. And naturally, when I retire, you will take over the business."

He made his way to the door and turned to speak to Clara again, "And you, my dear, are old enough to know your duties to this family."

Now, Lizzie was sitting at the table in the schoolroom, writing her daily letter to her mother. She thought of Clara, made to accompany her own mama as she sat in one drawing room after another and to make polite conversation with other young ladies, and understood that this was as unwelcome to Clara as stitching samplers was to her. She felt sorry for her eldest cousin, whom she admired greatly for her pretty face and kind manner. She was also full of admiration for Clara's ambition. Lizzie sighed as she bent her head over her letter again and went on writing: *Uncle William spoke a little today at lunch. He made a remark about Florence Nightingale. Clara wants to train in Miss Nightingale's new school for nurses, but Aunt Victoria does not approve and will do all she can to prevent it, I fear.*

I would like to do what Hugh says he wants to do, and travel the world looking for wonderful strange plants to bring back and grow here in

England. That would be wonderful, would it not? I think that if women can study to become nurses, they should also be allowed to study botany. Grandmama said that meals in the family were becoming as argumentative as a sitting of Parliament.

CHAPTER FIVE

Lizzie and Hugh disagree

After only a few days in London, Lizzie felt as though she were settling into the routines of the house. She still missed her mother. Even though Mama often sent letters, Lizzie wondered how life really was for her, alone with the gloomy Mr. Bright (whose name had always struck her as quite laughably inappropriate). But, for the most part, the time passed pleasantly enough. The lessons at Miss Jenkins's Academy were not difficult, but neither were they as interesting as Lizzie would have wished. Nevertheless, she found her classmates very agreeable. Lizzie and Lucy were accompanied to school by Elsie, the maid, who also met them and walked home with them after their midday meal, which they took at school.

The daily hour in the morning room (from three o'clock to four o'clock) was the worst time of the day for Lizzie. She couldn't understand why it was called the *morning* room when they generally frequented it after *lunch*. She and Lucy would sit with Aunt Victoria and attend to their handiwork. Lizzie looked often at the clock on the mantelpiece and wished the hands would move a little more quickly. This clock was much plainer than the one in the drawing room, which was in gold curlicues and twiddles. Also, in the drawing room, there was an arrangement of wax flowers under a glass dome, and many china figurines of shepherdesses in pretty skirts. These delicate creatures didn't look to Lizzie as though they'd ever been near a real sheep. She thought of Hugh, doing his sums and writing his compositions upstairs in the schoolroom, and longed to be allowed to learn the same things as he – his lessons were surely more interesting than tedious embroidery. She had glanced at his books sometimes when she had been writing letters, and had been intrigued to see the maps and diagrams and words in foreign languages.

Lizzie's sampler was now a little grubby around the edges, where she had gripped it so hard. Though her stitches were growing more even, they were still considered too large by Aunt Victoria, and she hadn't even finished the row of letters of the alphabet. There had been a good deal of unpicking. After the letters, there would be the numbers to complete and only then could she progress to the picture of a house and a tree. At her present rate of progress, it seemed as though she might never finish. At least when she was in her mother's care again, she would be spared this daily torment.

As soon as she had put away her sewing, Lucy ran out of the room. She was doubtless going down to the basement to talk to Cook and play with the cat, whose name was Mrs. Tibbs. When once Lizzie had suggested that she might accompany Lucy, she was told, rather firmly: "Mrs. Tibbs is my pet, and you can't touch her unless I give you permission."

Lizzie didn't want to play with Mrs. Tibbs today anyway. She had something else on her mind. When Aunt Victoria indicated that she was allowed to put her needlework away, Lizzie went to find Hugh. She had been so busy getting used to her new life in London that she hadn't had the chance to attend to the walnut she had brought with her from the country. The frost would soon be here, and the flowerpot needed to be outdoors, under some kind of shelter. She had discovered that there was a cold frame in the garden, which would do very well for her purposes. It looked like an enormous box with glass sides and a glass lid, which could be lifted up when the plants needed attention. A wizened old man named Amos Lewin came to tend the garden twice a week, and Lizzie had seen him, pottering about among the shrubs, often accompanied by Hugh. On one or two occasions, Lizzie had gone out to the garden while he was there, and tried to engage him in conversation, but he was a very quiet sort of man and for the most part she simply followed him around, looking at what he was doing and enjoying the sight of all the plants that he took care of. He was not at work today, but Hugh would help her to find the perfect place for her flowerpot.

Now that she was free of her wretched sampler, Lizzie flew up the stairs two at a time. Lucy was just on the point of going down to the kitchen and her voice reached Lizzie on the first landing.

"Mama would make you come downstairs and walk up again properly. She'd say you were a *hoyden*."

Lucy produced this last word with an air of great satisfaction.

"Then it's fortunate Aunt Victoria is otherwise occupied," said Lizzie, looking down at her cousin from the turn of the stair. Lucy tossed her curls and went down to the basement without another word. Lizzie ran up the next flight of stairs and opened the door of the schoolroom, and there was Hugh, drawing something very complicated in a sketchbook.

"Hugh?" Lizzie stood at his shoulder.

"Hmm?" Hugh was concentrating on his work and put down his pencil reluctantly. "I'm busy, Lizzie." He laughed. "Busy Lizzie. How very amusing…that's the name of a plant, don't you see?"

"I know. Hugh, I need you to help me, please. I have something that needs to go in the cold frame. I don't want Mr. Lewin to be put out by finding something unexpected in a place he's reserved for some other plant."

"What have you got? Where did you get it? You've hardly been out of the house, apart from going to school."

This was true. Lizzie had been on a few short walks, in the company of Grandmama, along the Embankment. She had visited *Frazer and Son* only a few days ago, together with Aunt Victoria and Clara, to buy a length of blue wool for a new dress that would be made up by Grandmama's own seamstress in time for Christmas. Now she said to Hugh, "I brought it with me from the country. It's a walnut, and I mean to grow it into a tree. I hope you will help me?"

"I'm sure your walnut would do better indoors," said Hugo. "The warmth of the house will help it to germinate."

"No," said Lizzie. "Mr. Alton, whose tree this walnut comes from, was most particular. The nut needs a hard frost to help it grow."

"Frost kills a young plant. Everyone knows that."

Lizzie wondered whether Hugh could possibly be right. He did, after all, spend a great deal of time reading about plants and animals, and she knew only what she'd been told. Perhaps Mr. Alton was mistaken.

Then she remembered the noble trees in the garden of his property in the village and knew that he wasn't. She said, "It's my walnut and I want to put it out in the cold frame."

"You're being stupid!" said Hugh. "You're just as obstinate as any other girl I've ever met. Girls never listen to reason. They don't know a thing about science."

"That's not true!" Lizzie protested. "I am *not* obstinate. I simply know what's right. I've been told by someone who's been harvesting walnut trees for years."

"When Mr. Lewin comes next week," said Hugh, "we can ask him, but I'm sure he'll agree with me."

"But I wanted my flowerpot to go outside this afternoon. Or tomorrow at the latest. Won't you help me? We can ask Mr. Lewin as well, but meanwhile…"

"You're the one who's going to cry when that nut doesn't sprout," said Hugh.

"Then you *will* help me? Oh, please do! I'm sure it's the right thing, truly."

"I can see that I'll be nagged and nagged if I don't do what you ask. You won't stop asking me, will you?"

"Certainly not. I shall continue till you give in."

Hugh sighed. "Tomorrow after school, then. I promise."

"Thank you. It'll be a wonderful walnut tree one day, you know. They grow slowly but they are very splendid when they're mature."

"Enough! I don't want to hear another word about your silly walnut. You're not only stubborn, like all girls, but also too fond of the sound of your own voice. Like all girls." Now that Hugh had promised to help her, Lizzie didn't mind his teasing so much, but she still picked up a book from the table and held it up in mock anger.

"Take back those rude remarks, Hugh, or I shall throw this book at your head."

Hugh burst out laughing. "I surrender! You're too fierce for me. I'm going to hide behind the rocking horse."

When Lucy came to call her brother and her cousin for supper, she found them chasing around the room, helpless with laughter.

"Whatever are you two up to?" she asked. "Lizzie looks a fright. Don't you think she looks a fright, Hugh? Mama will make you go upstairs again and brush your hair, Lizzie."

"Then I'd better go and do it before she sees me, hadn't I?" said Lizzie. She left the room, smiling at Hugh from behind Lucy's back.

CHAPTER SIX

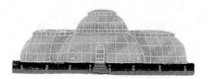

The family
visits Kew Gardens

On the following Sunday, which was the clearest, brightest November day Lizzie had ever seen, the Frazer family, all except for Uncle William, set out for Kew Gardens in the carriage. The horses had been specially brushed and groomed by their stable boys, in the livery stables where they were housed, and the Frazer family, Lizzie thought, looked just as fine. Everyone was in their Sunday best and Aunt Victoria's hat was decorated with pheasant's feathers. She had brought a gray fur muff with her, for there was a chill in the air. Grandmama had a fox fur around her neck, which Lizzie disliked intensely. The dead fox seemed to look out of his glass eyes most sadly.

"The trees will be magnificent," said Uncle Percy. "And there will be far fewer people than we might have met during the summer months. I can never understand why everyone so admires the natural world in May, June and July and quite loses interest in October and November."

"It's often very chilly during those months, dear," said Aunt Victoria, "and the flowers are mostly over by the autumn, are they not?"

Lizzie was staring silently out of the window. She looked at the river as they crossed Putney Bridge and could see the dome of St. Paul's Cathedral in the far distance. Her thoughts turned to her walnut, which was now safely installed in the cold frame. Even though he had complained, Hugh had helped her to find the right spot and it made her feel happy to think of it there, safe with the other plants.

She was relieved that she no longer had to worry about her flowerpot, for something else had begun to concern her. Up until now, every day had brought a letter from Lizzie's mama to her daughter. Lizzie longed for each delivery, and used to stand near the window of the front parlor, looking out for the mailman, who waved cheerily to her as he came to the door.

But for the last three days, there had been no word from Mama. At first, Lizzie was disappointed but not worried. It was possible that Mama was busy. Perhaps she and Mr. Bright had gone on a trip to visit a friend, though Lizzie found it hard to imagine who this might be. She determined not to fret, but as the days went by, it was hard not to imagine that something bad might have happened to her mother. The baby she was expecting was not due until the new year, but ladies, she knew, were sometimes unwell in the months before their babies were born.

She was determined not to say anything about it to anyone. Perhaps there would be a letter tomorrow. On this brilliantly sunny day, it was hard not to be optimistic and think that nothing was amiss. She was on her way to Kew Gardens, which Hugh said were the best in the whole world.

The gardens surpassed all Lizzie's expectations. The trees had lost most of their gold and scarlet leaves, but these lay about the ground in heaps, and the children crunched through them, shouting with delight. The wide paths between stretches of lawn were filled, on this fine day, with families enjoying the beauties of nature tamed. Clara and Lucy went off to walk with Uncle Percy round the lake and the others made their way toward an enormous greenhouse.

"This is the best thing in the whole of Kew," said Hugh to Lizzie. "It's just like a proper jungle in there. Let's go in."

The greenhouse was the most beautiful building that Lizzie had ever seen, and reminded her of the

Crystal Palace, where the Great Exhibition had been held. It was very high, with a curved roof that glittered in the sun, and all the beams and joints of the building were made of white wrought iron. She could see the dark green leaves of a plant she didn't recognize pressing against the panes. Aunt Victoria and Grandmama found a bench to rest on, and Hugh and Lizzie went inside.

The heat, the steamy air and the mossy, earthy smells in the greenhouse made Lizzie feel faint at first, but she followed Hugh up one of the paths, marveling at the lush greenery all around. At one end, a spiral staircase twisted up and up to the highest panes of all, and there were some trees that were almost tall enough to press against the glass roof. On a long trestle table at the far end of one of the gravel paths, an elderly gentleman was busy with pots and compost.

"Let's ask him," Hugh whispered to Lizzie.

"Ask him what?"

"About your silly walnut, of course. I'm sure it should be indoors."

"But we don't know him. Maybe he doesn't wish to be disturbed," Lizzie whispered back. Hugh wasn't listening. He had already approached the old man and was speaking to him.

"Good morning, sir," he said, and the elderly gentleman turned around.

"Good morning, lad," he said. "May I be of assistance? Mr. Samuel Hocking at your service."

"I'm Hugh Frazer and this is my cousin, Lizzie."

"Charmed, I'm sure," said Mr. Hocking and he bowed from the waist, with his fingers still covered with crumbs of dark brown earth. He looked, Lizzie thought, exactly like an elderly elf, being exceedingly small and red-faced, with a sparse, white beard.

"May I ask you a question, sir?" Hugh asked. "My cousin and I have been having a disagreement about a walnut."

"I'll help you if I can," said Mr. Hocking. "You are

trying to grow a walnut tree from a nut, I take it?"

"Yes, sir," said Lizzie, feeling braver now that Mr. Hocking had turned out to be so friendly. "I brought it to London from the country and I was told that it needed a hard frost to help it grow. Hugh says that warmth is good for plants, and indeed it is very warm in this greenhouse."

"Many of the plants here are tropical," said Mr. Hocking, "but you're quite right, Miss. A frost is just what's required. Perhaps there's a cold frame in your garden?"

"Yes, that's where we've put it," said Hugh.

"*You* thought it should remain indoors," Lizzie reminded him. "You didn't believe me, when I told you what Mr. Alton said."

"One should always, I've found, listen to the ladies," said Mr. Hocking.

"Thank you," said Lizzie. She made a face at Hugh. "I am going to plant it in the garden at the back of the house, when it's big enough."

"That will be delightful," said Mr. Hocking. "You should see some shoots coming from your nut early next year. Perhaps in February or March. They're slow to grow, are walnuts. That's what I love about these here…" He waved a hand at the variety of leaves and shoots that surrounded them in the jungle-like atmosphere of the greenhouse. "They grow up like Jack's beanstalk." He chuckled. "Yes, just like magic. Inches and inches almost overnight, it seems sometimes. But when it comes to walnuts, patience is the order of the day. Yes, that's it. Great patience."

The children said goodbye to their new friend and Hugh promised that they would return and see him on another occasion.

"Yes, indeed," said Mr. Hocking. "Now that I know about the walnut, I must be kept informed of its progress."

⟪⟫

While the family had been at Kew Gardens, and even on the drive back to Chelsea, Lizzie had managed not to think too much about her mother and what could possibly account for the fact that no letters had been delivered to the house recently. Once they reached home, however, and particularly once everyone had eaten supper and Lizzie was in the schoolroom with Lucy and Hugh, every kind of worrying thought began to come into her mind.

She wondered whether to tell anyone about her fears. Lucy asked her to join in a game of *Beggar my Neighbor*, but Lizzie had no taste for games. "I'm sorry, Lucy," she said. "I don't feel very much like playing tonight."

"Why?" said Lucy. "Are you ill? I shall tell Mama if you are."

"No, I'm well enough. Perhaps a little tired after our trip to Kew."

Hugh looked up from his chair. He was reading a book about the animals of the African continent, but he put it down at once. "I'm not tired," he said. "Even Lucy isn't tired. I think you're keeping something from us. You look strange, as if you're about to burst into tears. You're not, are you? I can't bear it when girls just start crying."

"I never cry," said Lucy, complacently. "I haven't cried since I was six."

"Yes, you have," said Hugh. "You cried when Mama sent you to your room for disobeying her, just the other day."

"I was angry, that's all. Angry tears don't count. They're not real tears, are they? Not like sad tears."

"I'm not sad," Lizzie said. "But I *am* a little worried. I don't know if I'm right to be, but I can't help it."

"Can't help what?" said Clara. She had come into the schoolroom to see whether the others were ready to prepare for bed.

"Lizzie's worried," said Lucy. "She won't tell us why."

Clara came and put her arm around Lizzie's shoulders at once.

"Oh, Lizzie dear, you really ought to tell! I'm sure that if you do, we can make you feel better."

"But I don't know whether I have good reason. If I

told you what the matter was, you'd think I was a fool."

"Tell us and let us decide for ourselves," Clara said. "I promise I shan't think any such thing."

Lizzie took a deep breath. "I write to Mama every day, as you know, and she has always written back at once. But for the last few days, there's been no word and I can't help thinking something must be very wrong. Perhaps Mama has been taken ill. Or perhaps there's been an accident...the baby..."

Talking about her deepest fears, putting them into words for the first time, made Lizzie feel even worse. Tears were standing in her eyes when she finished speaking, and she blinked them away.

"I'm sorry...I don't know why I'm crying exactly. Only I can't bear to think of what may be happening at home."

"I think that's quite understandable," said Clara. "Come with me now and we'll see what Mama and Papa say about it."

"Oh, no! I couldn't bother them with my concerns. They've been so kind to me already," said Lizzie.

"Nonsense," said Clara. "They undertook to look after you while your mother is indisposed. Papa would be mortified if you did not confide in him. Come with me, Lizzie. I'm sure there's something that can be done to reassure you."

CHAPTER SEVEN

Uncle William
speaks his mind

Aunt Victoria, Uncle Percy and Grandmama had finished their dinner and were sitting in the lamplight when Clara and Lizzie came into the drawing room. Hugh and Lucy remained outside the open door. They were, Lizzie knew, going to listen as best they could from there, for if all four children had burst into the room, they would certainly have been sent up to get ready for bed. Even Clara and Lizzie on their own were met with raised eyebrows from Aunt Victoria. The children were not permitted to come downstairs after dinner, except on very special occasions. Uncle Percy made a harrumphing noise, as though clearing his throat, and said, "Well now, to what do we owe the pleasure of this visitation? Lizzie, my dear, I should have thought it was nearly time for you to be thinking of getting ready for bed."

"Papa, Lizzie has something she wants to say to you. To ask you." Clara took Lizzie by the hand and led her to a spot on the carpet directly in front of Uncle Percy's chair. To Lizzie she said, "Go on. Tell Papa what you told me."

Lizzie wondered what everyone would say if she turned and ran from the room. Grandmama in particular was looking at her from behind the spectacles that she wore for reading with a rather disapproving expression. She was a great believer in proper bedtimes and she was frowning quite severely. If Uncle Percy hadn't taken Lizzie by the hand and said, "Come,

come, child. No one here is going to be angry with you, you know. Tell us what's worrying you, do," she would have made her escape at once.

Instead, she took a deep breath. "I have not had a letter from Mama for several days, and it's not like her at all," she whispered. "I fear that something may have happened to her. Or perhaps to the baby, and she doesn't know how to tell me in a way which won't distress me."

"Cecily has always been a very conscientious letter-writer, it's true," said Grandmama to Lizzie, "but it is also true that someone during the late stages of your mother's condition may be indisposed and therefore unable to write."

"I'm sure that Mama would put a few words on paper however ill she was," said Lizzie. "That is exactly why I…why I'm worried about her."

"I'm sure there's no reason to be frightened," said Uncle Percy. "I shall write to her myself and inquire. In a few days, we will know more, I feel certain. Go to bed now, my dear, and don't let it trouble you any longer."

Lizzie stood staring at Uncle Percy's feet, not knowing what to do. Only now, when she saw that there was to be *still* more waiting, did she realize how much she'd been hoping for immediate comfort. She felt so disappointed that her eyes filled with tears and she turned away to hide them.

Uncle William, who had been sitting silently up to that moment, suddenly stood up and strode over to Lizzie. She flinched a little and then immediately felt sorry, and wished she could have smiled welcomingly at her uncle instead. It wasn't Uncle William's fault that he looked so frightening, but it was difficult not to be somewhat scared of him. She had never, it was true, seen him lose his temper, but Lucy had told her stories of smashed dishes and curtains pulled from the window.

Uncle William wasn't interested in her, however. He came right up to Uncle Percy's chair and began to shout.

"You have no scrap of imagination, Percy. Can't you see the child is at her wits' end? What's the use of writing yet more letters and waiting and waiting? Don't you understand how endless the hours will be for Lizzie? Clearly, you don't. I refuse to stand here and let her go on and on being unhappy. I shall take the carriage as soon as possible…tomorrow morning… and drive Lizzie down to the country to visit her mama. I hope you all agree."

He glared around at the others. Grandmama looked as though she were about to say something, and Uncle William noticed this.

"Well, Mama? Do you wish to object?"

"No, no, my dear. I would only suggest that you wait until next Sunday, perhaps. After all, there is school to consider, is there not? We wouldn't wish Lizzie to miss her lessons, I'm sure."

"I don't care a fig for school and lessons and I have no intention of letting this child wait for nearly a week. She'll be worn out by the end of that time.

No, tomorrow it is. Percy, I may take the carriage, I presume?"

"I suppose you may, William," Uncle Percy said. "Are you sure you feel well enough for such a journey?"

"Well enough?" Now Uncle William was shouting again, even more loudly, and waving his arms in the air in a very alarming manner. "There's nothing wrong with me, except for the fact that I have lost an eye. I'm as strong as I ever was and I'll knock to the ground anyone who says different, that I will!"

"No one's suggesting that there's anything wrong with your health, my dear," said Grandmama, who seemed to be the only person in the family who could speak to William in a normal tone of voice. "I think Percy wonders whether you'll be able to remain calm enough when you arrive at Cecily's and make sure that you do not make any situation you find there even more…difficult."

Uncle William was suddenly silent. He looked

crestfallen, and for a moment, Lizzie thought he might begin to weep from his one eye. He did not shed any tears, however, but instead sighed deeply and said, much more quietly, "I shall be as gentle as a lamb, never fear, Mama. I'm sure I shouldn't like to frighten poor Cecily. Nor you, Lizzie," he added, addressing Lizzie directly for the very first time since her arrival in London.

"No, sir," said Lizzie, trying to compose herself and hide her fears. "I'm sure I won't be frightened at all. And it's most kind of you to take me to visit Mama. I will be ready in the morning. Thank you."

She bobbed a curtsey at everyone and fled from the room. Hugh and Lucy stood back to let her pass, and the three younger children ran upstairs together. When they arrived breathless on the landing outside their bedrooms, Elsie the maid was just coming downstairs from the attic to set the table for the next day's breakfast.

"You're very late to bed, children," she said, smiling

at them. "It'll be hard for you to rise and shine tomorrow."

"I'll be up at dawn, Elsie," said Lizzie. "I'm going to visit my mama in the country." She did not tell Elsie how nervous she felt at the prospect of being alone with Uncle William for the whole journey.

"I wish Uncle William would take me too," said Lucy. "I'd like to see the country. I've been to the seaside."

"I'm sure Uncle William has enough to worry about without having to deal with you too," Hugh said. "It's not going to be an outing, you know."

"I'm going to bed. You are the rudest brother that ever was!" said Lucy, flouncing into the bedroom. Lizzie followed her.

"Good night, Lizzie," said Hugh. "Wasn't it fun in the greenhouse today?"

"Yes," said Lizzie. "It was. I'd almost forgotten about it, what with all that's happened since we returned home. Good night."

Lizzie lay in bed, wide awake and listening to Lucy, who was snuffling a little through her nose as she slumbered. What she had said to Hugh was quite true. She *had* almost forgotten about Mr. Hocking and the wonderful plants he was in charge of. Hugh had pointed out to her the banks of rhododendrons, which came from the highest mountains in the world, called the Himalayas. Captain Hardwicke had first brought them to England in 1799, and more recently, Sir Joseph Hooker had added many other varieties from India. Hugh had also told her about the tulips they would see in the spring and how once, long ago, the bulbs were worth as much as jewels. How pleasant it would be to work in a greenhouse like a palace and care for growing things! Or even dig in the earth in the flowerbeds outdoors. How wonderful it would be to be a lady gardener! Thinking about this distracted Lizzie from what was really keeping her awake: a dread of the long journey to Mama's cottage (and back!)

with only Uncle William for company. What on earth would they find to say to one another? She hadn't been telling Uncle William the truth. She found that she was more than a little frightened having no one but him to speak to for hours and hours together.

CHAPTER EIGHT

Uncle William converses with Lizzie

"Are you comfortable, Lizzie?" said Uncle William, and Lizzie nodded. She was perched beside him on the high seat of the family carriage, because the day was fine, and she would have felt awkward sitting behind him as a passenger all by herself. Besides, she liked to look at the glossy chestnut backs of the horses. She wished that these beautiful creatures might live at the house, like Mrs. Tibbs, the cat, but she supposed that having horses grazing in the back garden would scandalize the neighbors. London was different from the country. There, everyone had fields near their houses where their horses could enjoy the open air, and the animals slept in stables nearby. But of course there was no room in London for every house to have a stable attached to it.

"Looking at the horses, are you?" said Uncle William, as he flicked the reins and they moved off. "Are you certain you are sitting comfortably, Lizzie? It can take time to get used to the motion. Fine creatures, horses. Understand every word you say to them. That's what I found, out in the Crimea."

Lizzie thought for a moment and then ventured a question. "Were you in the Cavalry?" She didn't know much about the Army, but she did know that the Cavalry rode horses and the Infantry had to march.

"No, not me. I had to walk across the battlefield. It made no difference, mark you. Bullets and swords find you wherever you are. But I did feel sorry for the poor horses, all the same. They never thought, did they, that they'd end up in a battle. They didn't know what was happening. Pitiful. It was enough to break your heart, seeing the unfortunate creatures with blood all over them, dead in the dirt."

Uncle William turned to Lizzie and added, "D'you know the poem by Lord Tennyson?

Stormed at with shot and shell,
Boldly they rode and well,
Into the jaws of Death,
Into the mouth of Hell
Rode the six hundred."

"*The Charge of the Light Brigade*…yes, we had to learn it at school."

"Lot of rot," said Uncle William. "Well, some of it is. Not the jaws of Death part. That's true enough. And the mouth of Hell, well, I hope I never have to see the real Hell, because if it's anything like the Crimea, then even the worst of sinners doesn't deserve such a fate."

"It must have been terrible," said Lizzie, partly hoping Uncle William would change the subject and partly fascinated to hear more. She had never met a real soldier before and she couldn't deny that however terrifying it was to think of dead men and horses covered in blood, however chilling it was to imagine the bullets whistling past your head and the swords slicing down all around you, there was also something exciting about the fact that the events Uncle William had witnessed were now part of history and there were even poems written about it, by famous poets like Lord Tennyson.

"Trouble with war is," Uncle William went on, "that people need to have heroes to worship. They need to hear stories about bravery and daring and victory. The other army needs to be thoroughly defeated and then everyone's happy. But I tell you, the real killer in the Crimea was disease. Disease and dirt. Cholera and dysentery killed more poor fellows than died in battle, I shouldn't wonder. But no one wants to read about sickness and dirt in their morning paper. No, they want glory!"

Uncle William sounded furious as he spoke. Lizzie wondered whether she dared to ask him about his missing eye. She plucked up her courage. "Uncle William, how did you come to lose your eye? It must have been so painful! I can't even think about it without tears springing to my eyes."

"Painful?" Uncle William fell silent for a moment. "I don't think anyone has ever asked me about that. Oh, don't mistake me. They're full of care and fussing around, but no one has asked me about the pain before. When my mother first saw me, when I came home from the war, she burst into tears, and Victoria fainted dead away. Dead away. Even Percy was silenced by the sight of me. I had a bandage around my head then, of course, and I was as thin as a skeleton after not eating properly for months. But I was alive. That was the thing that I clung to, through the pain. I was alive. So many others were lying dead in that wilderness.

But the pain. I don't know how to describe it. As though fire and rocks and biting creatures have taken up residence in your head. A tearing and a throbbing and a burning. Impossible to tell anyone what it's like, in truth. I don't have the words. Lord Tennyson would find it hard to describe, I'd warrant."

"How did it happen?" Lizzie wanted to know everything, now that Uncle William had started telling her about it.

"A bayonet wound. I suppose I can't complain, for the man I was attacking came off worse. I killed the poor fellow." Uncle William grunted.

Lizzie couldn't help it. She covered her face with her hands and shivered.

"Next thing I know," Uncle William continued, "I'm on a stretcher and being taken off to the hospital. And that I *am* glad of. She cared for me, you know. The Lady with the Lamp. Florence Nightingale herself. I'd be dead if it weren't for her. Everyone thinks of her as a gentle soul, an angel. Well, she was angelic and no mistake, but as tough as the most battle-hardened general as well. No one dared to disobey her. Woe betide you if she found dirt where it shouldn't have been. Cleanliness, that was the secret. Keeping everything clean, she insisted on that. She wiped my forehead. With her own hands. I had a fever, you see. For days and days I didn't know where I was, or who I was and she didn't give up. She wiped my brow and dressed my eye and held my hand and all the while I was having such dreams. You would not believe the strangeness of fever dreams. I saw monsters. Horses with tails made of fire. Fish with a woman's eyes. Men with their heads growing at the ends of their hands… Oh, I shouldn't be telling you this. It's not fit for a young girl to hear."

"No, it's as good as any story, Uncle William. Really. No one's ever told me anything like this before." A thought occurred to her. "Do you still have bad dreams?" she said. She felt shaken by what she'd been told, but didn't want to speak of her feelings.

"Often," said Uncle William. "Sometimes the dreams are so bad I'm frightened of going to sleep. So I stay awake too long and then I'm tired and cross during the day. Your cousins think I'm a very bad-tempered sort, and that's true, I suppose, but it's only because of the pain. I still have pains in my head. Miss Nightingale couldn't do anything for those, alas, though I don't get them as often as I used to. I must hope that I will mend entirely one of these days."

"Oh, I hope so most sincerely, Uncle William," said Lizzie.

Uncle William smiled at her. It was as though the sun had come out from behind the darkest of clouds. She realized that she had never seen her uncle smile before, not once. The sight warmed her.

"Your father's death...that was a blow to me, Lizzie," Uncle William continued. "Percy is a good man, but John was my favorite brother. And your mama...well, I always thought of her as a jewel among women. When you said you were worried about her, why, I found it impossible not to be worried myself. I would hate any harm to come to Cecily."

They had left London far behind them now, and both of them fell silent. Lizzie hadn't noticed the time going by, but she saw that they must have traveled quite a long way. The trees, some of them with all their leaves gone, were bending in the strong wind. Heavy, gray clouds covered the sky and the chill in the air meant that winter was truly upon them. Uncle William had tucked a rug around Lizzie's legs before they set off, but still she felt stiff and cold. She began to worry about Mama. What if she was lying ill in bed and didn't recognize her daughter? What then? Perhaps, though, all would be well. She thought longingly of firesides and the warmth that awaited them in the cottage.

As they drove at last into the village, Lizzie's spirits rose. Now that they were passing the Huntsman's Inn, now that they were coming up the lane to the cottage, her heart began to beat faster and faster. She was longing to see Mama and hold her and kiss her…

"Are you feeling brave, young Lizzie?" Uncle William asked. "I'm sure all will be well, but we'll be prepared, will we not? *Into the mouth of Hell*, like the six hundred, don't you know! Ready for anything."

Lizzie nodded, unable to speak. She had noticed that no smoke rose from the chimney of the cottage. Surely no one would neglect to light a fire in this weather. The carriage drew to a halt and Uncle William helped her to climb down. She didn't feel as if she were ready for anything. She stood beside her uncle as he lifted the brass knocker and let it drop onto the wooden front door. There was no answer, so Uncle William knocked again. Lizzie was just about to suggest that they went around to the back of the house when the door opened and there was Eli Bright, dressed, as always, in black from head to toe. He regarded Lizzie without smiling and then lifted his gaze to Uncle William.

"Good day to you, sir," Uncle William said. "I am William Frazer and I've brought my niece to visit her mother."

"I suppose you must come in, then," said Eli Bright, without so much as a single word of welcome or greeting. "I shall tell her you're here to see her."

He stepped into the dark interior of the cottage and Lizzie and Uncle William followed him. Lizzie was trembling. What would they find?

CHAPTER NINE

Lizzie and her mother are reunited

The interior of the cottage was so dark that Lizzie found it hard to make out the familiar furnishings and features of her old home. But there they were: the shabby armchairs next to the empty grate. Why had no fire been lit to take the chill off the room? The table still stood beside the window. It was covered by the plush cloth that Lizzie knew was almost as old as she was. The mantelpiece over the fire had nothing more decorative on it than a clock.

"To what do we owe this unexpected visit?" Mr. Bright inquired, looking as though the visit was far from a pleasure.

"Young Lizzie here was worried about her mama. She has not written for some time, and knowing that she is in a delicate condition, we were concerned for her welfare." Uncle William looked around the dark, chilly room and stared at Mr. Bright out of his one good eye. Lizzie, meanwhile, was edging toward the stairs. She could no longer keep silent. Her eagerness to be reunited with her mama was almost overwhelming.

"Is Mama upstairs?" she asked. "May I go up? And where is Annie?"

"I have dismissed Annie. Her wages were a drain upon the household. And besides, she was growing quite old and infirm. It was a kindness to her."

"But…" Lizzie was almost speechless with distress. "Why did Mama not tell me? How could you send Annie away before I could say goodbye? And how can

Mama manage all on her own? I want to see her. Is she in her bedroom? I must see her!"

"Your mother is resting. She is asleep, I've no doubt. Perhaps you would wait while I go and see."

"Nonsense, man!" Uncle William burst out. "Can't you see that Cecily would much rather be woken by her daughter than by anyone else in the world? How can you be so cruel as to make Lizzie wait after such a long journey? And you can see how distressed she is. Go on, Lizzie. He's not going to stop you."

Lizzie could see that Mr. Bright was taken aback by being spoken to in this manner. He took a step backward and let his mouth fall open in amazement. She decided to leave him to Uncle William, who would doubtless know how to deal with him. She tiptoed upstairs as quickly as she could, and knocked on her mother's bedroom door. There was no answer.

Lizzie stood outside on the little landing in some confusion. She hesitated to wake her mama, if indeed she was asleep, because everyone knew that when you were expecting a baby, you grew very tired and needed rest above all things. But Mama would certainly want to see her. Surely she's missing me, Lizzie thought, as much as I'm missing her? She decided to knock once more and go in.

The sight that met her eyes when she opened the door nearly made her cry. Her mother was indeed asleep, but her room was so bare and unwelcoming; the linen on the bed so sparse and shabby; the curtains at the windows so grubby and thin that as far as Lizzie could see, anyone who slept here would close her eyes the second she got into bed to avoid looking around. Was it, she wondered, that the room was always like this and she was only noticing it for the first time because she had grown used to the comfort and luxury of the house in Chelsea? Or had matters changed since her departure? She had only been gone a few weeks. Could such alterations happen in so short a time?

And her mama! Cecily's light-brown curls were in

disarray and looked as though they hadn't been brushed for a long time. Her mother's face was pale, too, and her lips, in the dim light of the room, had lost all color. If Lizzie hadn't known she was expecting a baby, she would have thought she was looking down at an invalid.

"Mama?" she whispered, touching her mother's shoulder gently. "Mama, wake up. It's me. It's Lizzie, come to see you."

Her mother stirred and opened her eyes. For a moment, she was silent, staring at her daughter, then she struggled to sit up.

"Lizzie! Lizzie, my dear! You're real! Oh, you're here. You're really here, my precious child. I thought you must be just another fragment of my dream. I dream about you so often…are you real?"

"Yes, of course I'm real, Mama." Lizzie flung herself onto the bed, and put her arms around her mother's neck and kissed her. The familiar smell, the smell of her mother's skin that she had known since childhood, was there, but overlaid with a kind of sourness, as though her mother had been perspiring under the bedclothes, or as though…could it be true?…she hadn't bathed lately.

As if she had been reading Lizzie's thoughts, Cecily said, "Oh, I must smell dreadful. It's such a business, heating up the water for a bath. And I am too weak to make the effort."

"But why?" Lizzie asked. "Why are you in bed the whole day? Is it because Annie is no longer here to take care of you? Oh, Mr. Bright is most wicked to send her away! Are you ill? If you are, we must call the doctor."

"No, no, not ill at all. Just the normal aches and pains of someone in my condition. And I stay in bed to save heating the parlor. We do not have a great deal of money. Dismissing Annie has saved us a little. But don't let's talk about that now. It's so wonderful to see you. How does it come that you're here? Is something wrong in London?"

"Uncle William brought me in the carriage. I was

worried about you. You haven't written for such a long time."

"I'm so sorry, my darling," said Cecily. "Eli persuaded me that too much letter-writing would tire me out, and only permits me to write to you once a week."

"That is the most dreadful thing I ever heard!" said Lizzie. "How does he dare to tell you when you can and can't write?" She did not dare to say so, but she thought that Mama might at least have written to tell her about Mr. Bright's decision, in order to stop her from worrying. She thought that this was easily the most wicked thing he'd ever done.

Tears stood in her mother's eyes, and Lizzie was contrite at once.

"I'm so sorry for shouting at you, Mama. I didn't mean it, really. And perhaps you are too weak to write to me. It doesn't matter about the letters. I will do without them if only I know you are well."

"You're a kinder daughter than I deserve, Lizzie.

And I will write in future, I promise. I will tell Eli that I will, yes. But now I must get up and greet your uncle."

Cecily pushed back the bedclothes and struggled out of bed. She said to Lizzie, "Go downstairs and wait for me there. I will dress and come down. You and Uncle William must take some refreshment with us. I'm sure we have enough to share, however humble it may be."

"I don't think you ought to cook, Mama. You don't look strong enough."

"You go down, dear. Tell Eli and Uncle William that I'll be there as soon as I can."

"I'd rather stay and help you to dress, Mama. Will you allow me to do that? I could arrange your hair."

"No, my dear, I'll be quicker on my own. You go downstairs, there's a good girl."

Lizzie went down to the parlor feeling quite powerless. Her heart was heavy when she considered how little she could do to help her mother.

CHAPTER TEN

Uncle William
takes action

Lizzie did as she was told. Down in the parlor, Uncle William was standing at the window, staring out at the small back garden, and Mr. Bright was seated at the table. Had they spoken at all while she was upstairs? It was hard to tell. She turned to Mr. Bright.

"Mama will be down in a moment. She says we're to take some refreshment with you."

"Indeed?" He didn't go on and Lizzie wondered

whether "indeed" meant that he was pleased or displeased at the idea of company for lunch. That was the thing that had most angered her about Mr. Bright. You never knew what he thought. His words were all of a piece: dull and flat and the very opposite of lively, whatever he wanted to say. She was wondering whether she had the courage to ask directly, when she heard her mother coming downstairs and stepping into the room.

"Cecily!" said Uncle William and he caught her up in a bear hug, lifting her off the floor and whirling her around as though she were nothing more than a child.

"William! How wonderful to see you! And in such good spirits, too. How are you?"

"Please," said Mr. Bright, frowning. "My wife is in a delicate condition. Your display of feeling is most unsuitable at such a time."

"Nonsense," said Uncle William. "Nothing I've done will harm either Cecily or her child." He turned back to Cecily. "I'm very well, I'm sure," he went on. He held Lizzie's mother at arm's length and looked very carefully at her. "Which is more than can be said for you, dear Cecily. You're pale, and you weigh not much more than Lizzie here, I'll be bound. Do you eat? Do you drink milk? Are you resting?"

"Yes, yes," said Cecily. "I'm doing very well."

"That's not what it looks like to me," said Uncle William. "What do you think, Lizzie?"

Lizzie was dismayed. Her mother's dress, when she compared it with the clothes that Aunt Victoria wore every day, was almost worn out. She remembered it from before she left the cottage, but at that time she hadn't realized that there were other dresses, other fabrics in the world which didn't have the weight and substance of a rag. Perhaps Mama was saving her good clothes until after the baby was born. She had arranged her hair and washed her face, but she was still just as pale and there were deep purple shadows under her eyes.

"You don't look like yourself, Mama," Lizzie said finally, not wanting to alarm her mother.

"Your daughter was concerned, Cecily," Uncle William added. "She wondered why you stopped writing to her."

"I've explained to Lizzie," said Cecily. "Mr. Bright has said that a letter once a week would be sufficient."

"Indeed, I did," said Mr. Bright. "Writing once a day is far too onerous for one in your condition. No one needs to write every day, I feel sure."

"That's not for you to decide," said Uncle William. "Although I can see that you have decided many things in this house."

"Cecily is my wife," said Mr. Bright. "I have a right to make decisions concerning her health and welfare."

"Health and welfare!" Uncle William was roaring by now. "How can even the most miserly of creatures find health and welfare in a hovel such as this? When my brother was alive, this was a place of comfort and ease and you have turned it into a kind of prison for

Cecily. In fact, I have seen prisons that are more luxuriously appointed than this."

Lizzie watched her mother as Uncle William spoke. She was sitting down now, on one of the two armchairs beside the grate and had covered her mouth with her hand. Mr. Bright was shocked into silence. Uncle William had just gotten into his stride, however. He marched into the tiny pantry, and called out over his shoulder, "Food! There is not enough food here to satisfy the mice! How dare you offer us refreshment when you know the state of your larder? Three eggs and the stale heel of a loaf of bread. Is this an adequate sufficiency for anyone? Anyone at all?"

"Today is market day," said Mr. Bright. "We will be going to buy our provisions later this afternoon. After your departure."

"Then you had best prepare yourself to go alone. Cecily, I am taking you to London with me. My brother's ghost would come and haunt my bedside if I left you here. Please go upstairs with Lizzie now and put a few necessities into a suitcase. We will be leaving shortly. We will lunch at the Huntsman's Inn."

"But…" Mr. Bright's composure was deserting him. He was opening his mouth to object when Uncle William growled, "I will strike you, sir, if you prevent me. If you wish to see your wife and child restored to you at any time in the future, I advise you to permit this short… holiday, let us call it…and raise no further objections."

"On the contrary," said Mr. Bright. "I feel Cecily will greatly enjoy a short stay with her relations in London. Her absence will allow me to save enough funds, perhaps, to make her life easier when she returns. We are, you see, very short of funds."

"Hmm," said Uncle William. "It may be that you are, but I cannot believe that you do not make enough money to keep you clothed and fed, at least. There's a great difference between abject poverty and purposely living as cheaply as one can. I know that my brother left enough money to provide for his wife and child.

Have you spent all that?"

"Certainly not. My wife's inheritance is safely in the bank. I was brought up to believe that one did not squander one's capital. There is such a thing as saving money."

"There is also such a thing as being a miser and a skinflint!" said Uncle William. "Go, Cecily. Go and pack your suitcase. You are coming with me and Lizzie."

The carriage was approaching London as dusk fell. The violet sky was studded with bright stars on this frosty night and, all over the city, lamps were lit and shining behind drawn curtains. Lizzie, who had fallen asleep for a little while after their good lunch of beef and roast potatoes at the Huntsman's Inn, woke up and looked at her mother. Already, even after such a short while away from Mr. Bright, Cecily was looking happier, although she was still pale, and getting ready for the journey had tired her greatly.

Lizzie felt content. All would be well, now that her mother was in London with her. They could forget about the chilly, comfortless cottage and the chilly, comfortless person who remained there by himself.

As the carriage drew up in front of the house, Lizzie said to Uncle William, "What will Uncle Percy say when he sees Mama?"

"Yes, William," said Mama. "It won't perhaps be convenient to have yet another person thrust upon the household."

"Look at this house, Cecily! Look at the size of it! Why, you could fit your cottage into it three times over and have room to spare. Percy and Victoria will be delighted. As for my mother, well, she likes nothing better than visitors and is forever complaining that we do not see enough company. Come, we will surprise them all."

He helped Cecily out of the carriage and Lizzie followed them up the steps. Now that they were at the house, she wondered whether indeed everyone would be as delighted as Uncle William said they'd be at the prospect of another mouth to feed and another body to accommodate.

CHAPTER ELEVEN

Lizzie's mama receives a letter

Lizzie was right. She couldn't say so to anyone, but she could see that when Uncle William turned up with Mama in the carriage, the family was somewhat surprised. Of course, they were all most welcoming and the house was certainly big enough to accommodate Cecily, but still, Lizzie knew that her arrival would mean something of an upheaval and, of course, there would soon be a baby and a nursery maid would have to be hired.

Uncle William told such hair-raising stories of the cottage and the behavior of Mr. Bright that everyone agreed he couldn't possibly have left his sister-in-law in such a situation. Uncle Percy simply said, "Well, all's well that ends well. That is all. Cecily is in grave need of support and shelter and we are happy to provide it. You're welcome, my dear."

On her first night in London, Lizzie's mother slept on a day-bed in the morning room, but the very next day the whole house was turned upside down, it seemed, as Aunt Victoria and Grandmama decided who was to give up their room for the new arrival. In the end, after much discussion, it was arranged. Cecily would have Lucy and Lizzie's room and the two girls would move in with Clara.

"I hope you're not too upset, Clara," said Lizzie, as she arranged her clothes in the new chest of drawers.

"I leave the grumbling to my little sister," said Clara. "She's the one who seems most put out. I am sorry not to have my own room any longer, but it can't be helped.

Hugh couldn't move in with you, and I don't think Uncle William would be comfortable in the attic, as he suggested. No, this is the best arrangement. After all, your mother will soon have a baby to care for, so she will need a larger bedroom than Hugh's in any case."

"It won't be for long," said Lizzie. "Mama intends to rest here for a few weeks and then return to the cottage."

As she spoke, she began to dread that day, but how was it to be prevented? How could she keep her mother here in London when Mama's husband was elsewhere and where, besides, she was creating so much inconvenience, whatever everyone said to the contrary?

Clara said, "She is welcome for as long as she wishes to stay, you know. For my part, I would love to care for a small baby. I am going to enroll at the nursing school next year, whatever Mama and Grandmama say. I've been persuading Papa of my unwavering desire to be a nurse whenever I happen to be alone with him and he's said that perhaps he would speak to them both. All nurses have to know about babies, do they not?"

"Yes, I'm sure they do," said Lizzie. "And you'd be such a good nurse, Clara."

For a few days after her mother's arrival, Lizzie quite forgot about her walnut, but when she remembered, she went at once to see how it had grown. Her disappointment when she saw that nothing had happened nearly made her cry. She resolved to be much more attentive in the future. So, every day, Lizzie went out to the garden and gazed into the cold frame, looking at the pot in which she had buried her walnut. She was beginning to think that maybe she had dreamed it all. It was hard to believe in a growing thing if it showed no signs of growth. All she could see in the pot was brown earth and more brown earth, and each time she visited the cold frame, Lizzie made a fervent wish, in the hope of persuading her walnut to grow.

"Please, little walnut, come out. Come out soon. You've been asleep for a very long time and you must wake up now. Please come out. Oh, I do wish you would!"

She made quite sure that no one was listening when she whispered these words. Lucy would have thought she was very silly and she did not dare to guess what Hugh would have said. Lizzie herself knew that it was not a scientific way to make plants come out of the earth, but she didn't think it would do any harm.

Shortly before Christmas, Uncle Percy received a letter from Mr. Bright. He summoned the whole family to the drawing room to hear what it said.

"I have here," he announced, "a letter from Cecily's husband, Mr. Eli Bright. I have already read it to Cecily and indeed she has received a letter too, with much the same information, though that is private to her, of course. I wish to tell you all what Mr. Bright says, because it will affect our life as a family and our future for the next few months at least." He coughed. "I shall read you the letter now: *Since my wife left me at the persuasion of your brother, I have been considering what is best for us all to do. I understand that life here is not as comfortable as it might be, but that is simply out of my desire to economize and my dislike of spending good money on frivolities. I believe that we all have too much luxury and that our reward for going without in this world will be riches in the next.*

Since Cecily is being cared for by you for the moment, I have taken the opportunity to put into action a plan I have nurtured for a long time. I am setting sail for West Africa in a few days' time, and intend to see whether the Church will be able to make use of me as a missionary there. Perhaps Cecily will join me in Africa when our child is old enough to travel safely to foreign parts. Until that time, I am grateful indeed that she has a family willing to care for her welfare and that of our child…"

Uncle Percy looked around. "The rest of the letter is not relevant."

Lizzie found that her heart was beating very fast. What did this mean? Surely Mama wouldn't think of going to live in Africa, even after the baby was old enough to travel. What would become of me, thought Lizzie, if she did? Uncle Percy was speaking again…

"I've considered this matter carefully and decided that we should do nothing for the moment. William will go down to the cottage and make inquiries about renting it out for the time being. When Cecily's child is born, and once the weather is warmer, we will see whether she can return to her home, with Lizzie and her new baby. But, until then, I am happy that we can give them a comfortable home. And, of course, it is out of the question for a very young child to travel to such an inhospitable climate. Mr. Eli Bright will have to resign himself to visiting England on home leave for the time being."

"Yes, indeed," said Grandmama. "I would not wish a grandchild of mine to go traveling about the globe in his infancy. Home's best and for the moment, this is your home, Cecily. I would not wish John's widow to lack for anything."

Lizzie thought that Grandmama's words were fine and kind, but her grandmother didn't look as though she relished the thought of this extended stay. Lizzie, however, could hardly believe her good fortune. It seemed that she and Mama would be living in London for the present. How strange it would be to have Mr. Bright so far away, and what a relief it would be not to have to see him in the near future. Maybe they would stay long enough for her to plant her walnut in the garden. She determined to ask Mr. Lewin, or perhaps even Mr. Hocking, if they visited Kew Gardens in the spring, when would be the best time to transfer her plant from the flowerpot to its proper home in London soil.

CHAPTER TWELVE

Lizzie has a sleepless night

Christmas was Lizzie's favorite time of the year. Mr. Dickens's story named *A Christmas Carol* was, she considered, a very fine book indeed, with its ghosts and the best ending of any story she had ever read. As the holiday approached, she grew more and more excited. All over the house, everyone was making preparations. Cook and Elsie had a huge goose, plucked and drawn and ready to stuff, lying on the wooden table in the kitchen; there was a fat plum pudding already made and waiting to be heated for the Christmas dinner. Grandmama herself had supervised the roasting of a gigantic side of ham, making sure that it was well-studded with cloves and basted with a spicy mixture of cinnamon, nutmeg and honey.

Uncle Percy and Uncle William had brought in a young spruce tree and installed it in the drawing room in a bucket which would, in the fullness of time, be covered up with a strip of wallpaper striped in red and gold.

"We'll be as grand as they are at Windsor Castle," said Uncle Percy, "with a tree that Prince Albert himself might well envy."

"May we help to decorate it, Papa?" asked Lucy. "Please say we may!"

"Only if you let Clara and Lizzie keep an eye on you to make sure that you don't eat all the gingerbread as you put it up. And the candles, of course, will be lit only when there are adults present. But yes, it will be a fine sight, I'm quite sure."

Lucy insisted on bringing Mrs. Tibbs the cat upstairs to see the ribbons and the pretty decorations Aunt Victoria had bought to make the tree beautiful, but Mrs. Tibbs was far more interested in the tempting smells wafting up from the kitchen and ran downstairs to where Cook and Elsie, in the indulgent spirit of the season, would allow her to eat the meaty scraps that had fallen onto the floor.

On Christmas morning, there were presents of fruit and nuts for all the children. Hugh and Lizzie each received a handsome wooden pencil case; Clara was given some pretty lace-edged handkerchiefs and Lucy a kaleidoscope.

Christmas dinner was a happy occasion. Lizzie was wearing her lovely new dress. The goose was roasted to perfection; the dessert was delicious and, by the end of the meal, everyone felt as though they never wished to eat another morsel ever again.

Cecily was sitting very upright in her chair and looking rather pale.

"Are you quite well, dear?" Grandmama asked, peering at Cecily through her spectacles.

"Yes, thank you. I believe I've eaten too much. A slight discomfort perhaps. It will soon pass. Indigestion, I suppose."

"Do you wish to withdraw?" Aunt Victoria asked.

"No, no," said Cecily and she tried to smile, but Lizzie thought that her mother didn't look quite herself.

"Let us raise our glasses," said Uncle Percy, just as Lizzie was wondering when they might leave the table. She wanted nothing more than to sit in the schoolroom and read quietly after all the rich food she had eaten. Hugh and Lucy were also looking full and red-faced and her mama, she could see, would have loved nothing better than to lie down in her bedroom. Still, Uncle Percy insisted on a toast. He raised his wineglass and said, "Health and happiness to us all. God bless us, every one!"

He winked at Lizzie, who recognized the quotation from *A Christmas Carol* and smiled back at her uncle. By the time the children were allowed to leave the table, night had fallen.

"Look!" said Hugh, when they were in the schoolroom. He had his nose pressed up against the window. "It's snowing."

"How lovely!" said Lucy. "Maybe tomorrow we'll be able to make a snowman in the garden."

Lizzie passed a very restless night. Perhaps, she thought, as she twisted and turned between sleep and wakefulness, I ate too much and my stomach is upset. I'm not used to such rich meat. Am I asleep? As she asked herself this question, she felt herself falling and falling and realized, even while she was dreaming, that she was, indeed, in a dream. There was banging and shouting somewhere far away and a voice saying, "Run! Be quick about it!" But no one she could see was running anywhere and the dream turned into one where she and Hugh were at Kew again, and the plants were growing all over the greenhouse like the roses around Sleeping Beauty's castle. Then the dream ended and Lizzie knew nothing further, till she heard Clara speaking quietly into her ear, and shaking her gently by the shoulder.

"Lizzie?" Clara said. "Lizzie, wake up. Can you hear something?"

Lizzie opened her eyes and saw that her cousin was standing beside her bed, with a shawl over her nightdress to protect her from the cold.

"Is it morning yet? It's still dark…" Lizzie said, drowsily.

"No, but listen. Can't you hear it?"

"I don't know what I'm listening for."

"I'm sure I heard a baby crying. I can't hear it now, but it woke me. Something woke me."

Clara gasped suddenly and added, "Your mama…it must be your mama. Perhaps she has given birth… But how is that possible? She was sitting at the dining table with us no more than a few hours ago. Surely we would have heard some comings and goings? Oh, but now I recall. Your mama thought she had indigestion during dinner. I suppose that must have been the beginning of her labor pains. Grandmama must have called the midwife, don't you think? Oh, Lizzie! We must go and have a look."

Lizzie got out of bed and found her slippers and dressing gown. She went to the door, which Clara had already opened. Sure enough, there were lights burning everywhere and Grandmama was standing outside Cecily's bedroom with her hair uncharacteristically in disarray. She had her sleeves rolled up and was wearing an apron over her gown.

"Grandmama, we heard a baby crying. Is it…?"

"Indeed it is!" said Grandmama. She came up to Lizzie and kissed her heartily. "You have a little brother, my dear. He gave no trouble being born; no trouble to speak of. Slipped out as though he couldn't wait to come into this world, even though we were not expecting him for a few weeks yet. We've washed him and your mother has fed him and she's resting now, but you may put your head around the door and peep at the little darling."

Clara burst out, "Oh, why didn't you call on me to help, Grandmama? I would have wanted to assist. You know how I love babies. And I've told you about my desire to be a nurse. This would have been a perfect opportunity for me to learn about childbirth."

"A baby being born is more than a lesson in nursing skills," said Grandmama, rather sharply. She went on a little more gently. "To tell the truth, dear, there wasn't time. Cecily went into labor shortly after you'd all gone to bed, and Uncle William ran down the road to fetch the midwife. I was in attendance; Cook and Elsie helped with the heating of the water. Everything was over before you could turn round. You will have plenty of opportunity to help from now on, you may be sure. Babies create a tremendous amount of work for everyone."

Lizzie opened the door of the room that had lately been her and Lucy's. She, too, was angry at herself for sleeping through her brother's arrival in the world. All the noises and shoutings she had thought she was hearing in her dreams must have been real. The curtains were still drawn and the bedroom was almost completely dark. In the light from the landing, Lizzie could make out a cradle, next to the bed.

"Mama?" she whispered. "Mama, are you awake?"

"Yes, Lizzie. Come and see."

Lizzie tiptoed to the bed and flung her arms around her mother's neck.

"Oh, Mama, Mama, are you well? I wish I'd woken up and then I'd have been here to help you."

Cecily laughed. "I needed very little help, I'm happy to say. You took your time being born but your brother was in a hurry to arrive."

"May I look at him, Mama?"

"Of course. He's sleeping soundly now."

Lizzie thought that she had never seen anything

half as beautiful as her baby brother. His little head was covered in soft, dark down and his tiny, tiny fingers were curled around the satin ribbon that bound the edge of his blanket.

"What's his name to be, Mama? What are we going to call him?"

"I have decided on John, after your papa, and William after your uncle. John William."

"Johnny," said Lizzie. "My brother Johnny. How I love him already!"

"I want you to do me a favor, Lizzie."

"Anything, Mama. I will do anything."

"Then please will you write to Eli? Tell him about the birth and that I am well and will write soon. Letters take a few weeks to reach him in Africa, but he must know as soon as possible. After all, Johnny is his son, too. Tell him about his child, and how beautiful he is."

"Of course I will, Mama," said Lizzie. She did not look forward to the task, but at least she would know what to say, and the letter did not have to be very long, after all. "I will write it this afternoon and show it to you before it's sent."

"Thank you, my dear. I can see how your eyes keep going back to the baby. He is handsome, is he not? I'm sure he will love you, his big sister, above everyone else."

CHAPTER THIRTEEN

The Frazer family
learns to live with an infant

On the afternoon of Boxing Day, the day that Johnny was born, Lizzie and Hugh and Lucy had gone out into the garden and swept up all the snow they could find to make a small snowman. Lucy had wanted the snowman to be a snow baby, but that was judged too difficult a task by Hugh and Lizzie and the ensuing argument had driven all three children indoors after a while. They hadn't returned to their half-made creature, and when the thaw came, it melted into the grass and was gone.

Since that day, three weeks had passed and the weather was dull and rainy. Lizzie had almost decided that her walnut was dead. Surely it ought to have appeared by now? All over the garden, snowdrops were showing their bright flowers in the grass and yet her walnut refused to grow at all. She felt very disappointed.

"Who would have thought such a tiny scrap of a child could turn a whole household upside down in less than a month?" said Grandmama, gently rocking little Johnny on her knee. Lizzie watched the two of them and thought that the time had flown by more quickly than she could have imagined.

The baby was swaddled in a cloth and had just been fed by his mama. Now he was in the morning room, being admired by everyone. Lucy treated him as an honorary pet, though she often remarked that he was not as entertaining as Mrs. Tibbs. "He doesn't do anything," she said. "When he is fed, he goes to sleep and when he is hungry, he cries and cries and we all have to take turns to walk him along in his carriage or rock him in the cradle. I hope he will become more interesting as he grows older." She did not sound optimistic.

"Young animals," said Hugh, "are much better at getting on in the world. Young cats or dogs can walk about almost as soon as they're born and they don't seem to need half the care and attention that human babies do. I wonder why that is. And feeding and sleeping are such a problem. Have you ever heard of a kitten who can't sleep?"

"I'm glad to say that Johnny is a good sleeper for the most part. Much better than you were, Hugh." Grandmama smiled at her eldest grandson. "I can recall you at this age, you know. I can even recall your papa when he was newborn."

Lucy laughed. "How funny to think of Papa in a swaddling cloth! I cannot imagine it."

"Nevertheless, he was. And so were you, Miss Lucy.

You were the most troublesome baby I ever knew and hardly allowed your poor mother a single undisturbed night."

Lizzie adored her little brother and looked forward to her turn to look after him. Mama had recovered well from the birth, and was now able to take her son out for walks and care for him, with help from the rest of the family.

Uncle Percy saw very little of the baby, because by the time he returned from the fabric shop, Johnny was generally asleep. Clara loved to wheel him down the road in his carriage and sometimes, she would wake up for Johnny's night feed, roused by his cries. Then she enjoyed going into Cecily's bedroom to help her change the child's diaper and settle him down after he had drunk his fill.

"I wish I could look after him instead of going visiting all the time," Clara used to tell Lizzie. "You are lucky to be with him every day."

"Yes," said Lizzie, though privately she thought that

Johnny perhaps demanded a little too much of everyone's energy. The baby was delightful, but no one seemed to have any time for anything except working to ensure his welfare.

The days and weeks passed quickly. Lizzie and Lucy and Hugh went to school every weekday. Lizzie had persuaded Hugh to tell her about some of his schoolwork, especially in mathematics, the sciences and geography, and she was learning many fascinating things: how plants germinated; how leaves became green; and how the clouds could show you what the weather was going to be like. It was finally a little warmer than it had been, but there were days when it was hard to believe that spring would ever arrive. It was still too chilly to hang the wash outside, and there seemed to be clotheshorses near every fire in the house on which various tiny garments had been draped to dry.

The walnut remained hidden in the earth in its flowerpot. As far as Lizzie could see, there had been no progress at all. She mentioned this to Hugh one evening, when the two of them were working on some mathematical problems at the schoolroom table.

"You're not going to see anything, Lizzie. Not till it actually sprouts. There will be nothing but dark soil to look at till it puts out a shoot. All the growing and so forth is going on underground. If the earth were transparent, you would be able to see changes, I'm sure."

"Yes, I know I would." Lizzie sighed. "I'm sure it will sprout one day, but I'm just saying it's hard to believe in it, that's all."

"Forget about it, Lizzie. Help me with this problem."

Lizzie turned her attention to the problem in which three men were digging a ditch and taking their time over it, as far as she could see. All Hugh's problems in mathematics involved three men, and they were always engaged in the most boring activities you could imagine. She wished very much that there was something in the house that she might do that would make her feel useful and calm the restlessness she felt.

Chapter Fourteen

Clara comes into her own

By the middle of February, Lizzie had become quite used to having a little brother, but was growing more and more irritated both with her mother and with Lucy. Despite her earlier complaints about his inactivity, her youngest cousin had grown more and more fond of Johnny with every passing week, and Cecily indulged her, allowing her to carry the baby and cuddle him just as though she were his sister, and not merely his cousin.

As soon as he opened his eyes – and sometimes even before that – Lucy was at his side, cooing and clucking and behaving in what Lizzie considered to be a really silly manner.

Hugh turned out to be the only person Lizzie could confide in about this. She didn't want to bother her mother; Clara was often out visiting with Aunt Victoria and Grandmama and, when she returned home, she, too, was absorbed in the baby. Lizzie didn't mind her attentions as much as she did Lucy's because Clara was a more sensible person and Lizzie could see that her mama relied on her help a great deal.

"It's probably my fault," Lizzie said to Hugh one day when they were in the garden together, looking at the crocuses that had just begun to poke their mauve and yellow heads out of the soil. "If I did more, then Lucy wouldn't have the opportunity to interfere so much. But though I adore Johnny, I do find sitting beside a cradle and pushing it backward and forward a bit tiresome after a while. Is that a very dreadful thing? Please don't tell anyone what I'm telling you, Hugh. I'm a little ashamed not to be a better sister."

"You're a perfectly good sister," said Hugh. "And I wouldn't let Lucy bother you. When Johnny's old enough to choose, he'll be happier with you. You can teach him all sorts of things, like running and climbing and everything I've taught you, too, which will be much more exciting for him than Lucy's nonsense. She hasn't got a thought in her head that isn't about dolls or clothes or tea parties. He's not going to be interested in those."

They were near the cold frame and Hugh added, "Let's take a look at your walnut."

Lizzie shook her head as they peered through the glass. "Nothing at all. Sometimes I think nothing is ever going to happen, but then I remember Mr. Hocking saying that we had to be patient. That is what I am being, though I do long for a sign."

She didn't add that sometimes she wondered

whether Hugh had been right all along and whether her flowerpot might have been better indoors, but she wasn't going to admit this to him.

When they had left the cold frame, Lizzie pointed to a spot in one of the flowerbeds.

"That's where I shall plant it," she told Hugh. "When it has sprouted and grown a little. Then, when we're long dead, there will be a fine tree here."

"Let us hope it sprouts, then," said Hugh. "At this rate, we'll be long dead before even a single green shoot appears!"

When Lizzie and Hugh returned to the house, they found everyone in a state of confusion. Uncle William was cradling little Johnny and rocking him back and forth in his arms. Aunt Victoria was comforting Lizzie's mama, who was weeping in an armchair, with her handkerchief pressed to her mouth. Grandmama was bustling about, telling Cook and Elsie what was needed for supper that evening, and when Hugh and

Lizzie came in, she turned to them with something like relief on her face.

"There you are, children. Now, there's not a moment to be lost."

Lizzie rushed to her mother's side. "What's the matter, Mama?" she cried. "What has happened?"

"Oh, Lizzie, it's poor little Johnny! He is not himself. No, not at all. He's not eating, and his face is flushed and hot and I think he might have a fever. Your grandmother is going to send for the doctor…oh, how I wish Johnny might be well again!"

"Let me go," said Hugh. "To fetch the doctor, I mean. I'll be there and back before you can blink."

"Yes, thank you, my dear," said Grandmama. "Run as fast as you can, and tell him to come at once."

Hugh had gone before anyone could say another word. Lizzie looked at him leaving the room and said, "I want to go. Please let me go. I can run just as fast as Hugh."

"I doubt that, my dear, but we won't argue about it

now," said Grandmama. "You may go to the shop instead and tell Percy and Clara, who went there only a short time ago, to come home at once."

Lizzie flung herself out of the front door and raced down the street in a fury. Grandmama has no idea how fast I can run, she thought. I shall show them. I shall show them all. She picked up her skirts and ran as fast as she could to the shop. As she went, she realized that Hugh had a far shorter journey to complete than she did. The doctor's house was in the next street and the shop was a good ten minutes' walk away. She didn't care. While she was running, it was hard to think of other things. All Lizzie's energies were concentrated on covering the ground as fast as she possibly could.

When she reached the shop, she almost fell into the door. Clara came around from behind the counter, and Uncle Percy found a stool for Lizzie to sit on, while her breathing returned to normal.

"It's Johnny," she gasped at last. "He's very sick, and Grandmama has sent me to fetch you both home."

For a little while, after the doctor had examined the baby and given him some medicine, matters became more peaceful. Little Johnny lay quietly in his cradle and Cecily, who was in the bed next to him, closed her eyes and fell asleep out of sheer exhaustion. The rest of the household hurried through the evening meal and then found they couldn't settle down to do anything. Even Lucy was subdued and went to bed much earlier than she usually did. By the time Lizzie came into the bedroom, she was fast asleep.

Lizzie lay in bed and closed her eyes. Please, she whispered – not quite sure whether she was praying to God or just wishing with all her heart – please let Johnny be well. I won't mind if Lucy cuddles him all day long. I won't care whether he loves me best or not. I'll take more care with my embroidery. I'll work harder at school. I'll be kind to everyone. Please let him be well.

Lizzie didn't remember falling asleep, but she

must have, because suddenly she realized that there was someone in the bedroom, speaking to Clara. She struggled to sit up and saw, in the light from the landing, that it was her mother, leaning over Clara's bed.

"Mama!" she whispered. "What's the matter?"

"Nothing, dear. I'm just speaking to Clara."

"But why?"

"It's Johnny. He's hot again. I don't know what to do. I didn't want to rouse the whole household, but Clara said…"

"I told your mama that she must wake me if the baby took a turn for the worse. The doctor is coming again in the morning, but he has instructed me in exactly what needs to be done, and I'm going to do it. I know just what Johnny needs." Clara had risen from her bed and was dressing hurriedly.

"How do you know?" Lizzie asked, but she was too late. Her mother and her cousin had rushed from the room. Lizzie wondered what time it was, and just then she heard the grandfather clock in the hall chiming three.

The very middle of the night! She'd not often been awake at this hour and there was a special kind of silence all around as though the whole world were muffled and blanketed. She would have welcomed any sound at all, even Uncle William shouting out in his dreams, or her little brother loudly demanding his night feeding. What was happening in her mother's bedroom? What was Clara doing? What did she mean by knowing what had to be done? Lizzie knew that she was wide awake now and she knew she would not fall asleep again. Her curiosity was overwhelming. She got out of bed, and put on her robe and slippers.

The door to Mama's bedroom was open. Lizzie peeked around it and saw that Clara had taken Johnny out of his cradle and laid him on the bed. She had removed all his blankets and he was dressed in nothing more than a diaper and a cotton nightshirt. Mama was sitting next to the baby on the bed, and holding him as Clara repeatedly took something...a cloth? It was hard to see from where Lizzie was standing... and dipped it into the basin full of water that stood on the floor next to her feet. Then she wrung it out and stroked it across the baby's forehead and arms and legs, over and over again, not stopping even for a moment.

Lizzie came up to her mother and said, "Oh, Mama! How worried you look! Is Johnny..." She paused. She couldn't say what she was thinking because it was so dreadful that even uttering the words would have made her cry. She wanted to know if her little brother was going to die, but couldn't ask. What if the answer was "yes"?

I won't be able to bear it if he dies, Lizzie thought. He's so small, he's scarcely even lived. It's not fair to let him die before he's had a chance to do anything... to walk or talk or play or go to school. And what will become of Mama if he's taken from her? Will I be enough for her now that she's had a son? That thought made Lizzie sadder than anything. "Can I do anything to help?" she said.

"No, thank you, Lizzie," said Clara, and Lizzie gazed at her cousin in astonishment. "All is well here. I am doing what needs to be done. Can you see? I am trying to make him cooler. He's too hot now. His fever is burning him up, poor little mite, but if we're patient and keep him cool with damp cloths, as I'm doing, then he'll soon be sleeping more peacefully. I've listened to Uncle William's stories of the Lady with the Lamp and how she used to do the same for the poor soldiers suffering from cholera and other terrible diseases. I am going to be a nurse, don't forget. This is what I shall be doing for much of the time, I expect. Fevers in childhood are very common."

Lizzie went to sit on the chair that her mother used to nurse the baby. No one needed her here, but she couldn't leave. She was too concerned about Johnny's health to go now, and she was soothed by Clara's quiet kindness and the way she betrayed not the slightest doubt that what she was doing was for the best. Why, she had even made Mama calm! That, surely, was a great gift to have if you wanted to become a nurse: the ability to give confidence to those who love the suffering person. At once, Lizzie relaxed. She would rest for a moment and then look at her brother again, to see if all was well. She closed her eyes and leaned against the back of the chair.

CHAPTER FIFTEEN

Lizzie has
two surprises

When Lizzie woke up, early morning light was coming through the bedroom curtains. Someone had covered her up with a blanket, but she felt chilly and stiff in all her limbs. She rose rather shakily to her feet and looked around her mother's bedroom. There was Mama, fast asleep on her pillows as though nothing worrisome had happened during the night. And there was the cradle with Johnny in it. Even from this distance, Lizzie could hear the whiffling sound he made while he slept. She tiptoed over to look at her little brother and saw him lying on his stomach, with his face turned to the right and one of his arms flung up above his head. He looked...Lizzie hardly dared to hope, but she reached out to touch him and found his skin cool under her fingers. Tears began to flow unchecked down her cheeks. He wasn't going to die, after all. He would live and run about and speak and she would tell him the story of how Clara had saved his life. Lizzie knew that her cousin would deny that it was her doing. She would say, modestly, that Johnny would probably have recovered on his own with no help from her, but perhaps he would not have. Lizzie determined to tell everyone in the family exactly what she had seen Clara do, and she intended also to ask Mama to mention it to the doctor when he came for his visit. Now, surely, no one could prevent Clara from enrolling in Miss Nightingale's school, not when she had shown herself to be such an excellent nurse. Lizzie felt so happy that she wanted to shout and rouse the household, but she knew it was much too early for that.

Where could she go? What could she do till breakfast? Her joy was like something bubbling up within her. She felt so wide awake that she couldn't imagine ever wanting to sleep again. She knew that Elsie and Cook always rose very early to prepare breakfast, so she decided to go down to the kitchen and see if they might give her a cup of warm milk. Mrs. Tibbs was doubtless still in her basket, and it would be pleasant to play with her with no interference from Lucy.

"Why, Miss Lizzie," said Cook as she came into the warmth of the kitchen. "Whatever's up, dear? Can't you sleep?"

"I woke up very early," Lizzie answered. "So I thought I'd come and visit Mrs. Tibbs."

"She's gone out. It's a lovely day, and she likes to trot about when the dew's still on the grass. Likes to wet her little paws…that's what I think. There she is, behind the laurel bush."

"I'll go out and fetch her," said Lizzie and she made for the back door before Cook could realize how ill-dressed she was. Fortunately, there was so much to do in the kitchen, getting breakfast ready for the whole family, that the small matter of one of the children going outdoors in her nightgown and bedroom slippers was the furthest thing from Cook's mind.

Mrs. Tibbs was picking her way delicately through the damp grass.

"Come here, kitty!" said Lizzie, and she laughed. No, Mrs. Tibbs was quite determined. She settled herself near the cold frame and looked at Lizzie as if to say: *I'm not moving. This is a good sunny spot and here I shall stay.*

"Well," said Lizzie. "Since you seem set on remaining here, I shall have a look at my walnut. Though I don't suppose anything has changed since I last saw it."

She lifted up the glass, and peered down at her

flowerpot. Then she looked more carefully and, still not quite believing the evidence of her own eyes, she picked up the flowerpot and examined it closely. And there it was: a tiny, green shoot, poking out of the dark earth all around it, and looking strong and vigorous to Lizzie, even though it was so small.

"You've sprouted!" she whispered to the little plant. "You're only a baby now, just like Johnny, but you'll both grow up strong and healthy. I know you will. Oh, what a wonderful morning this is!"

She put the flowerpot back in its place and closed the frame carefully. This was undoubtedly the best morning of her whole life. She knew that there was probably no connection (Hugh would say: *no scientific connection*) between the life bursting out of her walnut and the fact that her brother had been given another chance to thrive and flourish, but still she couldn't help linking them. She knew that as long as she lived, she would remember that the nut had put out its first greenness on the very day that Johnny recovered. Even when there was a sapling safely growing in the spot that she had chosen, she knew that she would be reminded of this day and of how happy she was. She felt as though every dream she had ever had might come true one day. She would have a lovely garden and work in it all by herself and bring thousands and thousands of plants into the world. And Johnny would help her. She would teach him exactly what he had to do.

Lizzie ran across the grass to the back door, not caring how wet her feet and the bottom of her nightdress had become, to wake the others and tell them her good news.

AUTHOR'S NOTE

When Linda Newbery, Ann Turnbull and I came together in 2004 to publish the Historical House series, we liked the idea of having the same house appearing in all our books. I was very happy that in this book, the heroine, Lizzie, plants a tree that grows through the other stories and is quite an old tree by the time the series ends.

This story is set just after the Crimean War and I was eager to show the advances that were made in nursing because of the work of Florence Nightingale and others. It was also a time of great interest in the natural world, and Lizzie's ambition to be a gardener reflects the excitement felt in Great Britain as explorers from all over the world brought back exotic plants and flowers to display in botanical gardens, such as Kew, which Lizzie visits in the story.

I hope you enjoy reading about her adventures.

Adèle Geras

About the Author

Adèle Geras was born in Jerusalem and before the age of eleven had lived in Cyprus, Nigeria and North Borneo. She studied languages at Oxford University and taught French before becoming a full-time author. She has written more than ninety books for children and young adults, including *Troy*, which was shortlisted for a prestigious UK children's book award, and its companion volume, *Ithaca*.

She lives in Cambridge and has two daughters and four grandchildren.

To find out more about Adèle Geras, you can visit her website: www.adelegeras.com.

USBORNE QUICKLINKS

For links to websites where you can find out more about Kew Gardens, Florence Nightingale and the Crimean War, and life and fashion in Victorian times, go to the Usborne Quicklinks website at www.usborne.com/quicklinks and type in the title of this book.

At Usborne Quicklinks you can:
- See inside the Victorian glasshouse at Kew Gardens
- See a paper lamp used by Florence Nightingale
- Find out more about the Crimean War
- Find out how a Victorian Christmas cake was made

Please follow the online safety guidelines at the Usborne Quicklinks website.